AN EMPTY CHAIR

AND OTHER STORIES

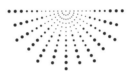

Edited by

THE YOUNG AUTHOR PROJECT

AN ANTHOLOGY OF SHORT STORIES
By the students of Guildford County School

PUBLISHED BY
THE YOUNG AUTHOR PROJECT, MARCH 2019

Copyright © 2019 Guildford County School/Young Author Project

FOREWORD

By Cara Thurlbourn,
Director of the Young Author Project

The Young Author Project team and myself want to say a massive, 'Congratulations,' to all students from Guildford County School who are featured in this fantastic anthology.

We were truly impressed with the standard of submissions but, most of all, we're thrilled that so many young people were passionate enough about writing and stories to want to take part.

Each student clearly worked very hard on their story submission. However, we felt that special mention should go to 'An Empty Chair' by Evie Tear. The anthology's title and cover were inspired by her work.

The Young Author Project is designed to show young people that if you're passionate and you work hard, anything is possible. The students from Guildford County School have certainly proved that this is true and we sincerely hope they are proud of their achievements.

CONTENTS

An Empty Chair, *Evie Tear*   1

A Change in Poppy, *Lauren Horton*   4

A Fresh Start, *Levi Ayres*   8

A Love Story, *Nicole Werry*   10

A New Chapter, *Evie Beech*   14

A Style of My Own, *Coral Leadbetter*   17

A Change of Diet, *Josh Thompson*   19

A Desperate Salvation, *Stanley Pillay*   22

Aftermath, *Ollie Cork*   26

Assumptions, *Isobel Kirkwood*   29

Change, *Zeb Baker*   32

Colours, *Eleanor Cook*   35

Coward, *Sophie Laycock*   39

Crimson Red, *Gabriel Glynn*   43

Dead Girl Walking, *Phoebe Ship*   46

Death's Change, *Ben Mallia*   51

Thud, *Lauren Mcintyre*   54

Finally Loved, *Grace Mitchell*   58

For VALA, *Eleanor Daniels*   62

The Ghosts of Grief Lake, *Madeleine Davies*   67

'Guilty', *Martha Tizard*   71

Hero, *Maya Clowes*   74

Hide and Seek, *Jasmin Goharriz*   77

High Risk Change, *George Simms*   80

It's Always the Kids' Fault, *James Ward*   83

Long Noses Kill, *Oscar Drage*   86

Lost, *Maya Patel*   90

Magic, *Lily Hobbs*   94

My Boots Squelch in the Mud, *James Garner*   98

Noise, *Molly Chatwin*   101

Normal, *Cal Darragh*   104

One Orange, Two Green, *Rosie Relph*   108

Pangea and The Great Samurai War, *Leo Mack*   111

People Like Me, *Annabelle Shaw*   115

Poppies, *Kenzo Patch*   118

Remembering, *Emma Shepherd*   121

Safe Passage, *Erin Gruenberg*   124

Six Feet Under, *Holly Banwell*   127

The Best Day of My Life, *Matilda Billinge*   131

The Cure, *Sophie Myers*   134

The Fossil, *Tom Walsh*   137

The Inheritance, *Isabelle Currey*   140

The Journey, *Maggie Patmore*   143

The New Sicily, *Sofia Cosgrove*   147

The Search for a Star, *Violet Isaacs*   149

The Storm, *Dillan Turner*   152

The Top Hat, *Catherine Speirs*   156

The Magic Sofa Bed, *Lily Borthwick*   160

Trapped, *Joe Williams*   164

Flatline, *Amber Neil*   167

The Abyss of the Moon, *Charlie Newman*   171

Acknowledgments   174

About The Young Author Project   175

AN EMPTY CHAIR

EVIE TEAR, YEAR 7

*L*ooking behind me, I see the empty chair, feel my longing to be with her. Filling my nostrils, pursuing me, is the smell of colour and hope. However, the smell of hatred lies beneath, choking me, like a black ugly river coated with pretty white bubbles, like a storm smoothed over with fluffy white clouds. Her smell.

Tick tock. Tick tock.

My eyes wander around the room aimlessly, before looking down at my scuffed, black brogues. Every so often, I peer around until a pair of sad, miserable eyes glance towards me and I look down. Outside, it is not raining. Though it is not sunny either. It is a dull, grey blanket, like the sky is speechless, like it doesn't know what to say.

Yet, the sun beams at me, at the edge of the sky, like a light at the end of a tunnel – a tunnel to the end of suffering.

Glimpsing around the room, eyes twitch, noses wrinkle, lips are nibbled, feet tap. My mind is all a blur. And then suddenly, I can see her everywhere, laughing and joking around. She takes my hand and we run up onto our beautiful, luscious, green hill where we sit and watch the milky, drifting clouds until our eyes water with the complexity of it. Gazing into her azure eyes, knowing that ...

"Excuse me!"

I am back. There is only so far my mind can take me away from this treacherous world. Thinking back to yesterday – a day of innocence ruined by the face of evil. We sat side by side in the classroom, laughing and giggling and enjoying each other's company. Miss was being unusually kind to us: now I understand why.

Stomp! Stomp!

Everyone sat up straight; everything all of a sudden felt tense and uncomfortable. Silence. A young man opened the door and strode towards the front of the classroom. As he saluted, he sternly snapped two words, breaking the silence: "Heil Hitler!"

Then he paced up and down between our wooden, varnished desks, looking at us like a lion does when it chooses which one of the frail, agile antelope he would like for dinner. As he wandered back to the front of the classroom, I gazed down at his black, shiny boots, which clicked when he pressed his heels down. My teacher tiptoed towards him like a bird sneaking around an alligator. In a whisper she murmured a few soft words in his ear. However, to this, he raised one eyebrow and shook his head at her. His stare made me feel shaky – for it was the uncertainty of this curious man that put me on the edge. Although he seemed so tough, I could see the fear in his eyes, see him biting his lips. Then he bellowed for her. Her skin turned pale. She gulped and stood up, her hand shaking. Shuffling towards the door, her eyes met mine – we knew that this was goodbye. Goodbye to my friend forever.

I know that she is gone but in my mind she lives on. But I have missed the last train, the train that pulls us together. And, now I have missed it, she is slowly fading into the distance of my memory as I sit and stare at the empty chair.

A CHANGE IN POPPY

LAUREN HORTON, YEAR 9

The floor swayed beneath my shaken, ice cold toes. Eyes like daggers from every angle, it felt like everybody was seeing through me. Each classroom wall narrowing closer and closer, I could feel my rapid breathing hit back onto my flushed face. I looked down at my hands for some sense of recognition. Clammy palms, bitten nails, home-work reminders, scarlet knuckles. I forced my non-existent nails into my hands: distract, distract, distract. It hadn't sunk in yet, I began to feel cold and numb and guilty and... and now I was crying and screaming inside. I stormed out and the eyes of my fellow class 'mates' followed my every move. A welcoming breeze hit my arms, which were covered in goose-bumps for quite a while.

Although it's not much better than the classroom, I reached the bathroom filled with a, somehow relaxing, dead air.

Placing my hands on the toilet sinks for balance, I glanced at my unrecognisable self. The face I once called mine was unflattering and colourless. And the previous tears stained my cheeks and fought through my drug store foundation.

"She's gone." Mum, 11:04am

"Don't freak out. Poppy was really happy when you wanted to meet her, but she's worried what you'll think," Mum admitted, the fear in her eyes revealing her true emotions.

A month ago, I would have told you a summery dress hugged her healthy figure and the bright summer tan complimented her look, and her golden hair coiffed into neat ringlets.

Now, the washed-out hospital gown over hung on her slender limbs, some lifeless hair remained on her empty head. Blood-less and veiny skin had wires and tubes and who knows what else going into the petite body. The look on my face gave away that I was terrified, confused, upset, and guilty, and Poppy couldn't look me in the eye.

Mum shared a tender hug with her and gave her the adventure books that we used to read in the tree house that Dad made, where we would dream of escaping this average town and become famous explorers. On school nights, we'd sometimes sneak out to the park opposite our house and climb the tallest trees and view the glowing town.

But now she was trapped in these four walls, she doesn't know if she can walk, if she can leave, if she can get better, and if her childhood dreams could ever be pursued. She must watch people walk by, smile, laugh, enjoy the outdoors play on the swings, climb the tallest trees.

5

With a fake smile plastered onto my face, I ran towards the form of my sister that I could only fear of seeing.

"Whoa, whoa, slow down!?" Mum warned, guarding Poppy.

Poppy splurged on about the food, and the late nights, and the cool outing that the doctors promised she would get. She had met some lovely friends who had been diagnosed with similar difficulties and they have occasional meetings where they discuss what sandwiches are the best.

"I want to hold people like I used to," Poppy sighed. "It's not the same anymore."

The words hit me like a tonne of bricks, the shock had robbed me from speech, I was motionless.

"Me too..." I agreed, I didn't know how to reply. "So, you said there was good news!"

"Twelve days, twelve days!" Poppy squealed as she revealed the calendar and the days she crossed off with a sparkly red pen (her favourite colour). "Once this last operation is over, I'll be free to go! Go home and see Fad and all my friends at school. I wonder if they still remember me."

"Of course, they do!" I reassured, flicking through an album of photos that she'd taken.

That was the only time I saw her in hospital. Twelve days, twelve days, twelve days. Mum tried to make me go to see her, but I couldn't face Poppy with the new image she owned. I had to sit and watch her be in pain, there was no way I could do that. The doctors knew that there was a low chance of success with the operation, but they didn't want to tell her because her dreams seemed to become the truth. They let her believe that one day she could run around in the playground at school and learn again. For twelve, she wrote in her joyful journal with upbeat stories of traveling the world.

The doctors told her there was a high risk that the operation would fail, that didn't stop Poppy's hope. Then the upbeat stories stopped, and the occasional meetings, and the discussing of ice-cream flavours.

All that was left was a book filled with hopeful stories in world left with no hope.

A FRESH START

LEVI AYRES, YEAR 9

The loud cars, the buildings, the pollution… the city is so populated. I feel nervous and overwhelmed. I'm used to seeing trees above me, now it's just bricks and concrete. Car horns and people shouting. I smell the fumes from the trucks and it tastes gritty in my mouth. People barge into me, trying to get down the narrow street.

How am I going to live here? How will I ever get to sleep with all this racket? Home for me is blue skies, grass, sheep. The smoke from the open fire in my cosy cabin, the fresh clean air of the meadows. The sounds of the rustle of leaves and the trees swaying in the wind. The cows' soft mooing and my two dogs, Joe and Tony, wagging their tails, happy from running in the fields.

I'm never going to get used to this, I hate the city and everything about it. Joe and Tony will have nowhere to run around. I wish that the day to move from my cabin had never come.

I had packed up my possessions in the boxes, my furniture had already been put on the removal van.

As I stood looking around I felt really angry. My lovely cabin that I had built from scratch was going to be demolished to make way for a large housing estate.

As I looked through the window, I could see the bulldozer and other large machines waiting to get started. I noticed the engine was running on the bulldozer and the driver was nowhere to be seen. I ran over and jumped in. I drove the machine right through the middle of the cabin. It collapsed like a house of cards and I was left in the middle of the debris feeling sad. As I climbed out, the driver ran over and took the keys as we both looked around at what was left of my cabin.

I went over to my 4x4. My dogs, Joe and Tony, greeted me with wagging tails, licking my face.

A LOVE STORY

NICOLE WERRY, YEAR 9

*B*efore entering, she examined her appearance: fading coiffed hair, combed and tucked tightly in place, a tint of red that struggled to grasp on the cracking remains of her lips. Her eyes, blank and distant. Her fingers gently brushed mournfully over her once-beautiful porcelain skin, now a slab of leather. Rough to the touch and an eyesore to others.

"You will love me again. You want her? I will be her, anything you want," she pleaded silently.

Her fingers constricted around the image tightly, as if it was her ticket to eternal happiness. The golden locks cascading down her youthful shoulders, full lips that looked as if no other soul had ever touched such a delicacy. Her silky-smooth hands, having not done a day's work in her life, clenched on to the snow-white pearls that hugged her neck. No speck of dirt ever crossing the boundaries of her grace. Yet, all Emilia witnessed was a soulless woman. Gazing at the photo, she was consumed by her thoughts.

He will abandon her in the remains of her youth and allure. He will leave her distraught and used and worthless. No longer a delicate rose, untouched and beautiful. All he will see are her thorns, the petals grasping to the little colour, life and finesse that remains. The way he views me. The light will shift, I will be her, I will be youthful again. That was what she craved. But...

In a flash, she was back there.

The day repeats, circling her mind as if she was compelled to endure the worst moments of her life. Again. Again. Again. Every single time she felt as if she was going to be sick, the emotions and grief bubbles up to her throat, waiting to explode. Every. Single. Time. Clenched fists, distraught with rage, turmoil and sorrow. Sweat smeared along her palms and the nape of her neck. Struggling to hold in tears, no longer able to retain them, they leak. Everything around her seemed to suffocate her, whether it was the chair cushioning her or the sleeper hostile mattress that patrolled her every breath of the day. The makeshift, plastic mirror that consumed so much of her time, made the sight of herself slant to the right ever so slightly, the type of mirror used in her childhood vanity. The windows guarded by large iron bars, far above the mattress reliant on the rusty, metal bed frame. Letting a slight glimpse of the outside shed into the bare, concrete room.

The ironclad door slowly rasps open, revealing a man, draped in a pale blue uniform, the blank expression on his face comforted her. The sight of him reassured her it was Wednesday, Emilia whisks off through the corridor, passing tens of the exact same door that clung to her room. At the end of the elongated path, there stood an opening. As she enters, her eyes scan a man, so familiar. His grey plaid blazer dangled from the chair, loosely hanging to his frigid body. His eyes examined hers, his face paralysed to the same expression. She sets herself down on the battered leather chair that was facing him. The man's monotone, droning voice bored her. The clock echoes through her ears, eyes trailing off to his head, shiny, smooth and no hair to be found for miles. The carpet scraped against her foot, the sound of her breath distracts Emilia until slowly she returned back to reality.

"Emilia," he abruptly announced. "Tell me again, your love story."

As she happily narrated the best year of her life, she stopped. After witnessing Dr Alton's expression, "What?" she demanded.

He hesitantly replied, "The real version Emilia..."

She shut her eyes, a stream of memories overflowed through her mind. David and Janet meeting each other's eyes across the classroom that first day of college, their first magical kiss, the sentiments they shared and all the memories they made. Such happiness, then suddenly pain struck. Her heart piercing. Discovering the deception, the secrets concealed from her, rage and greed taking over. Her golden locks no longer cascading but dismembered on the ground. Her bones consumed with vengeance. Her full lips, blue. Her hands sliced left from right, no longer soft as silk. It was necessary for Janet to keep him to herself.

She was now a soulless woman.

A NEW CHAPTER

BY EVIE BEECH, YEAR 9

*a*s we rolled up in our battered car, my hands started to sweat and my legs started to tremble.

The huge black gates loomed over me as I stepped out of the car. I grabbed my dilapidated bag and my checked lunch box, shouted goodbye to my parents then slammed the door shut. This was it, my first day…

The halls echoed my every move and it was dead silent, you could hear a pin drop. Where was everyone? There are graffiti drawings all over the grey lockers and a thick layer of dust along the top. Most of the classrooms where locked with not a single person to be seen. The lights flickered and creaked and were covered in cobwebs.

At the sound of the bell, the atmosphere changed which causes the butterflies to come rushing back from when I was getting out of the car. There are big, tall kids as well as small, little kids shouting and screaming.

Because I came late into school, I missed the first two lessons in the morning and it is now lunch. The queue for the main meal snakes round the corridor and into the library. In the canteen there are six tables but seven if you include the staff one. The tables are split into different types of people: popular, nerdy, weird, quiet, musical, and sporty. I don't know where to sit but I have a packed lunch and no one else does so I am a bit nervous and scared. After about two minutes of trying to make myself look as invisible as possible, I decide to sit in the cold damp toilets and each my lunch quietly and alone. The pipes around me are very squeaky and make a lot of noise. The cubical are very narrow and the walls are green, covered in writing and most of it is inappropriate. After about ten minutes, I have finished my lunch and pluck the courage to venture outside but when I do the halls are flooded with people, again!

I look down at my timetable and unfold it to find what class I have, which is English in A19. I realise I only have two minutes and I have no idea where my class is. I walk around vigorously trying to find the classroom, but I only have one minute now. I start to panic and stress because it is a very big school (with also five floors) and there are about 40 class-rooms, do I go to the office and ask?

Suddenly, I feel a hand on my shoulder... I turn around. Half blinded by tears, my eyes are fixed on the floor, I see a pair of black shoes, white checked socks, black skinny jeans, a blue t-shirt, and a black baseball cap.

"Are you new? My name is Sam."

A STYLE OF MY OWN

CORAL LEADBETTER, YEAR 9

oday's the day, the day I can finally get a change. The door creaks open with the bell ringing. A soft voice says, "Take a seat." I shift over to the seats and sit down. Putting my head down, my tangled hair covers my face while I look down at my sweaty hands. I lift my head up and I look around. I'm surrounded by young children and babies screaming. I place my head back down into my palms, hoping everything would just happen quicker and it would just be quiet. I just want it done, I just want it to be over, I hate this tension. Suddenly I hear heavy footsteps coming my way, I lift my head up from my hands and look up. A tall man with star gazing blue eyes. His voice sounds like a dream. As he says, "Hello, what can we do for you today?" I can't help but fall into his eyes

I've always been the quiet one, the not so smart one, the less popular. I've always been compared to my sister, Millie. She's always been the popular one, the intelligent one, the better twin. We were always dressed the same, same clothes, same hair style. Since starting school, I've always wanted a change but I've never been allowed. The teachers never really liked me because I wasn't like Millie and I wasn't sporty enough. I've always been compared to her and how I needed to be as intelligent as her and as sporty. I've never been that girl and I don't want to be; I'm sick of being compared. I have always preferred to read books, while she's always doing sports or hanging out with friends. That's why I've had a change because I'm never going to be her.

I hate it. It's so short, I don't even recognise myself. The flow of my long silky hair is gone. Its flat, stiff, it does not move, why did I do it… but I know I'll get used to it… at least I can't be compared anymore. I'm different. Not the same… never going to be the same anymore. This is the new me: strong, independent, clever. That's me.

A CHANGE OF DIET

JOSH THOMPSON, YEAR 9

The bright white wall turned a pitch black as the switch was pressed. His sandy yellow hair flew down the creaking stairs, they squealed as any sort of weight was put on them. Smooth, sky-blue walls, newly painted, went past like a blur. The new paint smell was everywhere. Peeling flakes of paint drifted from the ceiling like discoloured snowflakes. The old mahogany counter was the best of the kitchen, the silver ear-piercing blender and a rusty toaster resting on Phil's counter. Flickering lights shone on a stained yellow cupboard, which would have once been white.

Phil's legs ached; his forehead was sweaty; he wanted, just wanted to get into the first team so much. All Phil needed to do was get slightly fitter but he was not patient, he needed to do something else to get fitter. His legs drove his tired body on left, right, left, right. He had to get up onto that gigantic hill;

he would not give up at anything. Now sweat was dripping like a waterfall from most parts of his body. His luminous green Adidas hoodie reflected on the silver Honda that he just passed. Phil's black laces which once tangled together were now loose. The top of the hill was near but his body felt like he was about to collapse.

The creek of the chair burst the silence of the new day and Phil had cooked his first vegan meal. He really didn't want to go vegan but he had no other ideas on helping him get fitter, he had been doing running but he needed a bigger change. The dish lay below the dodgy flashing lights, unappetizingly – vegetables thrown into the pretzel bun – it did not at all look appealing. Vegetables overflowing like they were trying to escape, well more like they needed to escape. The first bite was forced into the rock-hard, ageing bun and he was struggling to break it down. After ten minutes of force feeding himself, every last bit of food was down his mouth and into his stomach.

The next morning, Phil's sandy yellow hair flopped down on his newly shaved sides of his head. His stomach had been growling since he got up. He pulled up his navy-blue track suit bottoms with the football club emblem on it that he has seen his whole life. Phil glided down the stairs, grabbed his banana, which was slowly turning green to bright yellow, from his mahogany counter and took his thick smoothie that was blended last night. Next, he shoved the creaking door to its normal self. As he started to run on the concrete pavement the blur of the blue bus – he used to catch.

His stomach begun to rumble again and he realised that this veganism was never going to work.

A DESPERATE SALVATION

STANLEY PILLAY, YEAR 8

*H*ome. I wanted to be home more than anywhere. But no. My aircraft's engines had frozen over and stopped. But why, God, oh why did I have to land in Scotland?

I crawled out of the smoking wreckage that was once my plane and sprawled face-first into the snow. I struggled to a stand and surveyed the surroundings. Snow, as far as the eye could see. I had known that the nuclear winter over the British Isles was bad, but I hadn't known that the bombs had rendered it a wasteland...

I trudged over to my plane and tried in vain to open a flap on the fuselage. Peering around, I spied a long, thin piece of metal that had fallen from the wing. I used it to pry open the flap, revealing a small camo green backpack. Ripping it open, I found some provisions, a survival blanket, and some matches. But as I put the bag down, I heard a faint but fast *clickclickclickclick* coming from it. Again, I rifled through the pockets of the bag and discovered a small metal box that had turned on when I had put the bag down. Realising what it was, I began to feel panic well up inside of me. It was a Geiger counter, the type which measured radiation. And it was going crazy…

I held the counter up to my face and inspected the little dials on the face of the box that would tell me how quickly I would die. The red needle was frantically head-butting the end of the dial. This was bad. Really bad. I shot over to the seat of the plane and yanked the silvery-white radiation clothes out from under the mangled, twisted seat. These would keep me safe for now. I knew the closest safe zone from the radiation was London, and that was several hundred miles away. The clothing's proofing would last three weeks, according to the label. So, around fifteen miles a day, at bare minimum pace. I had done hiking before, but this was something else. Fifteen miles a day, sleeping in snow holes in-between? That was madness.

A week into the gruelling trek, I found my first trace of what used to be life. My feet were pulverised, and bleeding in places. Every bone in my body ached, screaming for me to stop, to just sit down and die… but I kept walking. And so, after a week of nothing but pain and misery, I found a small village. It seemed like nobody was still there, as it was deadly quiet. They were probably in a safe zone, or dead. But as I stared, transfixed, at the ghost town, I realised; we had caused all this. It may have been the Russian Empire that had ordered the bombing of the British Isles, but they had been eradicated as a result of siding with us, the new Americans. And we had started the war.

Left foot, right foot, left foot, right foot. Over and over, over and over. Each footfall was agony. Falling over was getting more and more frequent. Stumbling over roots, sprawling in the snow. Every time, I got up. Until now. I just lay, staring up at the grey sky, letting the darkness cover my eyes…

It would be easier to just let go… easier just to…

"Wake up! Wake UP!"

I awoke to a man shaking my shoulders. I was no longer wearing the radiation clothes, and I was lying in what looked like the attic of a wooden lodge. "Oh, thank God, you're alive! We were beginning to think you weren't going to wake," he said, clearly very relived. "Come downstairs when you feel hungry, we've got food to spare." He clambered down the ladder.

I sat upright and gasped with the pain coming from… well, coming from everywhere, really. Climbing down the ladder, I smell food. I staggered down to the table, with a bowl of porridge sat on it. I ate it like it was the best food on Earth. As I ate, the man waked in, and briefed me on their situation. He and his children had not had the money to move to a safe zone, so had radiation-proofed their house and hunted for food wearing radiation clothes. Oh, and they couldn't go out of their house because of the radiation, and the infected people staggering around the remains of the town. I had a plan on how to get out of the town, but I had a snowball's chance in hell of making it.

The very next morning, I got up early. I, for possibly the last time, donned the radiation clothes, and walked to the front door. I opened the door and ran for my life.

AFTERMATH

OLLIE CORK, YEAR 8

*T*he ground was still shaking, my ears were still ringing, and my body still felt like hell, but I found the power to scream, "Milo." No response. My body started to rush with fear and adrenalin. I screamed again, somehow even louder, "Milo!" Nothing. I then looked around. Parts of the bunker had collapsed and the rest was unstable. I had to get out.

Two hours before...

"Everyone into bunkers nuclear strike imminent." I heard a lifeless robotic voice say. And I knew what it meant, sprinting as fast as I could until I reached a concrete set of stairs, I called for my family as they ran towards me. When we had all reached the stairs, we ran down one by one as we had been told to practice once a week by the Government (I always thought we were wasting our time doing it every day after school on a Monday but, clearly, I was wrong). When we got to the bottom of the spiral stairs me and my brother Milo closed the colossal bulkhead door. We survived, but for how long?

The next few minutes were terrifying, my family (sat in the bracing chairs) was silent. A minute felt like an hour and the second hand on the clock made me flinch every time it ticked. Then I heard the robotic voice again, my heart stopped. "Brace, brace, brace." Then, before the sound even registered in my brain, I was unconscious. Tha's how I found myself calling for Milo.

I looked above me and I could see the rebar in the concrete bent and snapped. Then slowly and painfully I got out of my bracing chair and looked at the rest of my family, I was the first up or last alive. I moved as fast as I could to the chair next to mine. I looked. It was my dad plus a piece of shrapnel in is chest. I knew he was dead, but I still shouted, "Dad! Wake up, please!" Tears started to stream down my face, but I knew there was no time to mourn his death.

I then walked over to my brother. He looked fine apart from a cut on his arm from God knows what. Then, just to make sure, I checked his pulse – it was beating. I called his name at him until his eyes fluttered open. "Wha… what happened?"

I smiled. "We just survived a nuclear attack!"

Slowly, I helped Milo out of his chair. He looked pale tired and lifeless but still managed to stand up. I filled him in on the news about Dad and how the whole bunker could collapse at any minute, he looked terrified. Looking at Mum, we knew she hadn't made it, she had been ill for about two years and doctors said she could not survive anything worse than falling over.

Milo and I moved towards the bulkhead door to the bunker. It didn't look good. The handle had snapped off and the door was still sealed. I pushed at the door as hard as I could, but nothing happened. I collapsed, my body was full of pain, sadness and drained of energy. Although there were tools and provisions that could last us a lifetime, it was hope that we needed. After rummaging through the supplies I found the tools that could get us out: a sledge hammer and a pickaxe. I called for Milo to take one and we hit the door for three hours straight. By the time we had finished, we had made a hole through the concrete door that we could fit through. Adrenalin rushed through our bodies excitedly we climbed through and walked on the rubble that used to be our house and through the door.

All I saw was death and destruction and the dust made me choke. There was a man in front of us. He was dressed in a suit and his face was cold and blunt and he started clapping, saying harshly, "You have made it past the first stage. Well done."

ASSUMPTIONS

ISOBEL KIRKWOOD, YEAR 7

Savannah Wishmonger looked at the wedding ring on her finger and felt agitated. Was this the end of her and Roy's relationship? They had once been so close, but now she felt he was very insignificant in her life. It couldn't be over so soon, could it? They had only been married for one year! He was such a nice man – they were a perfect couple, everyone said so... maybe he wasn't the love of her life after all.

Savannah had met Roy in secondary school. No, it wasn't love at first sight, actually, quite the opposite. Roy had been a nuisance at school: detentions all day, late homework – sometimes no homework at all! It was only a few years after secondary school that they met up again on an Architectural Design course. He had completely changed.

A few years could change more than just appearance; personality too! Roy had gone from ignorant and dismissive to kind and caring. She had approached him one day with her eyes glued to the ground and her hands flat by her sides, trying to make sure he wouldn't recognise her. But... he did... his reaction was somewhere along the lines of, "Hey Savannah! Haven't seen you in a while!" Savannah had decided to give him the benefit of the doubt, but never had she expected that they would end up married.

She had suspected (for a couple of months now) that Roy had been having an affair with another woman. At the time, it had seemed like a perfect answer for the unexplained nights out and random phone calls... now she wasn't so sure about it.

She had considered many other reasons, but Savannah thought this one was the most likely.

On Saturday morning, 13th September, the Wishmongers got up like normal. Eating her crispy croissant on the sofa, Savannah read the newspaper. On the front was another murder report, that was the fifth one this week! Roy sat opposite Savannah on the armchair with his feet up enjoying his freshly-squeezed orange juice. The sofa creaked as she got up and a spring dropped onto the carpet. She observed the peeling wallpaper. The crippling debt she remembered she was in made her cringe.

After breakfast, Savannah went outside for a refreshing walk. The stones crunched under her boots as she wandered along the footpath. She needed to build up the courage to interrogate Roy. The smell of sweet honeysuckle reminded her of her own sweet, carefree childhood. The warm sun glared down on all its surroundings. Why couldn't life always be like this?

What could she ask him..? Savannah wasn't the bravest of people and that didn't really help the situation. Her brain was whirling with unstable thoughts. She examined the chipped lilac nail polish on her finger. Thinking about her and Roy's future relationship, she removed her phone and dialled his mobile. She imagined him still sitting on the armchair. Maybe it would be easier not speaking to him face-to-face. No answer. Letting out a sigh, Savannah returned home.

Later that night, Savannah was taking a shower when she heard the front door shut and she realised Roy had slipped out without saying where he was going. It was another one of his unexplained nights out – typical! With a towel wrapped around her head, Savannah slouched down on the sofa and a few more springs popped out. The stars twinkled in the night sky. Where was the moon? She stood up and stumbled over to the window.

There, stood over a dead body, was Roy, with a gun in his hand.

CHANGE

ZEB BAKER, YEAR 7

They lay silently, cuddled into the crooks of their warm cave-like home. A car horn swept past, stirring them from their deep slumber. They had been undisturbed for many a day and had caught up with much needed sleep. A noise of anger and brutality arose from somewhere behind. Possessing rough skin, a hand entered their chamber clawing around, searching for anything it could acquire.

As it did so, a thin sliver of light licked the bottom of the now open crevasse, revealing the drowsy residents. Unable to fight, all they could do was look on as their relatives were taken away from the warm familiarity of home.

As their heads breached the surface, a rush of odd smells attacked them: a perfume that was too strong; a burrito that lay sadly on the sidewalk; and a flea infected cat that seemed to hop-scotch down an alley. As they were yanked up higher their tails dangled below them, swaying in the oncoming breeze, sirens launched above the sounds of the bustling area, making the hand – which was now quite comfortable – release its grip. As they clattered onto the hard rock which was the pavement, a large bird swooped in and picked up the greater amount of the bunch (it must have been quite a clumsy bird, mistaking them for a quick snack). The rest left to lay on the busy streets of New York.

They flew quickly but not elegantly, dipping and ducking around branches, whilst small gaps that were unknown to man proved no difficulty for the speeding bird. A friend plummeted from the beak causing a hum of chaotic noises. It landed in the middle of a caterpillar nest disturbing the pregnant mother. She reared up, thinking that it was a predator, but she experienced a moment of disbelief as it didn't attack.

They came to a stop above a park, quite a large one actually. It had a big lake with rowing boats bobbing around on its glass like surface, a play-area and benches (for worn out parents tired of their children's screams). For around a minute, they hovered at the dizzying height until the bird arched down towards the park, coming to a halt underneath an old kids' swing.

A loud boy, no older than five, came charging at the swing. He was armed with an ice cream in one hand and a little red ball in the other. The bird looked curiously at the ice cream, as drops slipped from the rounded top and fell onto the floor. If no other animal came those small drops would potentially be its family's next meal. As it rushed to tell this great news, the now saliva-covered disks dropped from its beak landing with a thud on the tartan-cushion flooring. The now ice-cream-covered boy jumped in surprise at the objects that lay on the floor. After he'd got over his mild shock, he started a mad rush to pick all of it up. As his meaty fingers gripped around them, they finally got it into their heads where they were heading. Home. Home, sweet home. A place they hadn't been for what seemed like an eternity. Whilst they sank down deeper into the boy's over large pocket, they finally realised how much they had missed it. Now they were back to their old self, pocket change.

COLOURS

ELEANOR COOK, YEAR 9

ONE YEAR AGO

The sun is dying, as it does every day, leaving the world on its own. To most people this death is beautiful, in varying colours of pink and red and orange. However, these colours mask the truth. They paint this death as a wonderful spectacle for all to watch, when in reality death is not a good thing. It is immoral and deadly. It eats everything in its path, leaving only destruction and chaos. When it's done, lives are left destroyed and people are left alone, isolated. These colours disappear as soon as they came.

NOW

I'm next to my sister, watching the colours dance across the sky from where we are sitting amongst the white wildflowers on top of Aine Hill. It was breath-taking. The way they raced and twirled, chasing each other, illuminating everything in their path, including the city far below where we are now lying. Up here, above the world, there is a sense of peace. This place is so detached from the rest of earth, you can no longer think of anything that could worry you. That's why we love coming up here, especially seeing as mum no longer can.

ONE YEAR AGO

As the colours fade, the world turns grey, appearing lifeless, yet I'm the only one who can see it. Alone, standing up here, nobody can see me, nobody can hear me and no-one is here to witness this cold city with me. Far below me I can see as slowly lights flicker on in each building of the city, one by one. It's starting to get colder now the sun has gone. My long, unkempt hair is flung harshly at my cheeks by the wind as it sweeps past, stirring up the decaying leaves which litter the frozen ground around my shoes.

NOW

The colours slowly finish their race across the midnight sky allowing the city under us to once again bask in the cool evening air. As most of the natural light drifts beyond the horizon the maze of buildings comes to life. Wrapping a soft blanket around my sister's shoulders, I leaned closer to her so we could both stay warm. Although there was a faint wind running through the flowers sprinkled around us, my shoulder-length hair remained resting on my shoulders making sure my ears didn't get too cold. I haven't been back here since I cut my hair.

ONE YEAR AGO

I don't know how long I've been staring unfocused, lost in my thoughts, subconsciously pulling my battered jacket further around me. It's not like anyone is going to notice I'm not at home, they haven't for the last however many days I've stayed, crouched among the crumbling leaves and brittle grass, through the never-ending winter nights. The harsh wind continuously beats my face, reminding me that I shouldn't be here, that I should be at home doing homework or studying or maybe even playing piano. Not that I've been able to play since the hospital. Flashing lights. Machines whirring and beeping, demanding attention. Doctors, surgeons, yelling. Hushed voices. Tears.

NOW

We should start walking back soon, it's getting late and I have to wake up to drive back to university tomorrow. I'm also playing in a concert on Tuesday so I have to get back to rehearse; for now, though I will continue in this moment. City lights. Rustling of the leaves in the trees swaying back and forth, humming to each other. Wildflowers, fireflies, surround us. Warm blankets. Smiles.

ONE YEAR AGO

The sun has completely set now, leaving everything, yet again, as it always will.

NOW

The colours are gone now, but they will be back tomorrow and the next and the next day... forever.

COWARD

SOPHIE LAYCOCK, YEAR 9

*F*ear is like a ravenous animal; it can sense your fear and when you're at your weakest it attacks.

The day started off like any other Monday morning. I wake up late to my mum shaking me and whispering, "Stella!" Scrambling about, I get changed, constantly bumping into my sweat and shaving foam scented brothers. I end up leaving my house wiping off the white sticky froth smeared over my freckled face.

Destiny and Nina are waiting outside. While Nina gives me a lecture, Destiny hands me a cereal bar, knowing all too well that I forgot to have breakfast.

I let Nina persuade us to take the short route to school which basically consists of a field and a small pathway. Unluckily it rained all last night, so the field is a melted ice lolly with mud gushing over my foot with every step I take. Nina smiles smugly, peering down at her laces, while me and Destiny end up sprinting down the field with our slip-ons drowning in mud.

Finally, we get to the cobbled dusty pathway leading to school. After recovering from the retching with the others about the thick sludgy mud, I notice something. There are no mothers juggling babies on their hips, no business people striding about in their polished suits, I hear no cars whizzing about, any other people are gone. My friends notice it to, they notice I'm scared (as usual) so they talk unnaturally, almost forced, to cover up the deadly silence. I trail behind them as we turn the corner.

I freeze. My brain is telling me to move but every bone in my body is cemented to the spot. Outside my school are 20 or so people stood with huge guns, I don't get a chance to see their faces before I'm grabbed and flung into a powdery pile of cement in someone's front garden.

Destiny and Nina tower above me checking I'm okay and then run further down the garden and try to open the door. I sit up, my breath getting heavier. Betty, a girl in my year, walks past, headphone in her ears. I hiss at her like the others but it is no use, she continues bopping to school. My friends are too far away to reach her in time, so they beckon to me to go out there and get her, to save her. I attempt to get up. My whole body is trembling with fear. "You'll only be in eyesight for a second," I tell myself. But I can't do it, I'm not brave enough. I hear a nauseating gun shot, I wipe tears that are surging from my eyes and bury myself in the soil.

I lie in the soil for four hours. My lungs are encased in the lumpy substance. Something grabs my foot and I try to shriek but I end up puffing up soil. My friends tug on my arm and I follow them, barely looking up because I can't bear to see the disappointment on their faces. We stumble through people's front gardens to get to the forest for four hours. My knees are cut, my arms are bruised, my face is stained with tears. But we make it.

Pine leaves jab at my back as I wake up violently. I hear sticks crunching under someone's weight and the panting of breath. I get up gradually ready to yelp at any second. a boy and a girl in the year above us are staring intently at us: they are some of my brother's friends (Owen and Georgina). I wake up Nina and Destiny and we gather in a circle. Owen and Georgina tell us what happened.

"Trumps had a plan, a stupid plan. He believes all teachers should carry guns to protect us, so last night he gave every teacher a gun," Owen began.

Georgina butted in. "But our school's teachers have gone mad with power. It corrupts people and they were no exception. They're holding most people captive in the school, but not everyone made it." She looked down.

"We escaped, before it was too late." Owen paused, looking at us.

I thought of Betty. How could I have been such a coward? Because that's what I am: a coward.

"I have a plan and we will save them." Everyone stares at me in awe. I may be a coward. But I will die fighting to be brave, rather than live a life as a coward with a never-ending feeling of uneasiness in my stomach. I will be brave.

CRIMSON RED

GABRIEL GLYNN, YEAR 8

Sabrina opened her eyes…

The moment the shuttle door opened, Sabrina Musk knew how her dad felt when he stepped onto the brutal surface of the planet of war… Mars. No mission had ever survived the journey, so being the realist that she was Sabrina didn't have high hopes for anything better.

With sand swooping against her visor, and glorious sunbeams glaring her eyes, Sabrina took a deep breath and stepped onto the red planet. Instantly, something just didn't feel right, was it the eeriness of the wind, or the cave that seemed to lurk on the edge of her vison. With all the courage summed up inside of her, Sabrina started to gingerly walk towards the lurking cave.

It gave off a strange scent, almost like… "Blood!" Sabrina shouted. It was everywhere: oozing off the walls; dripping off the ceiling. "This isn't normal, none of this is," she whispered quietly, only wishing it was a friend she was talking to, and not herself. Palms sweaty and heart beating like a drum, Sabrina started to sprint out of the hideous place when suddenly a thumping noise erupted, it was growing louder and louder by the second, not wishing to know what it was and only wanting to get back to the shuttle, Sabrina didn't dare to turn around even when she could swear she felt breathing on the back of her neck…

The sprint felt like an eternity, every second of it haunted by that… thing, but finally Sabrina could see light, and relief warmed its way through her body. Pivoting at the edge of the cave, Sabrina whipped out her pistol and pointed it towards the mouth but there was… nothing, only the pitch black chasm like there always was. *Did I imagine that whole thing?* Sabrina thought to herself?

Later that afternoon, Sabrina busied herself with forgetting the whole experience by collecting underground soil samples to send back to the research lab. But that was when she noticed it: an eye. A big red devouring eye at the mouth of the cave. Sabrina gradually stood up and walked slowly backwards to the safety of the shuttle. She had barely made one step before the creature pounced, but Sabrina was quick and made it back in time to the shuttle where she locked the door and gulped. She had never seen anything like it before: 8 foot tall; coal black scaly skin; two claws the size of scythes and a face, a mangled face with a singular eye planted in middle of it. *What have I got myself into?* she thought, as the creature pushed over the shuttle as if it were no more than a piece of rubbish beneath its feet

There was no hope now and Sabrina knew it. As soon as she would step outside, that thing would tear her to pieces. Nothing could save her, this was the end. With rivers of tears streaming down her face, she said her final goodbyes to the people she loved. Maybe now she would be reunited with her father. Sabrina's hand reached out and pulled her gun from its holster. She pointed it towards her head and pulled the trigger, and with that she closed her eyes.

DEAD GIRL WALKING

PHOEBE SHIP, YEAR 9

*I*solation so crippling could eat a man alive. It is much like ice – frozen forever in time, in a distant region, cut off from the rest of the world. Crystallising, derelict, hidden from the kind rays of sunlight.

Clean, white hills surround a glistening, isolated lagoon. Pink, blue and yellow blend into a magnificent artwork of sky, creating an aura of peace – yet eyes can be deceiving. Thundering waterfalls gently crash onto a sheen blanket of illuminating ice, trapping the dark depths below.

Trapping the dead girl below.

Wisps of her white dress encircle her flawless, once-brown face. Now, her skin glows pale with an enchanting blue haze. She floats like a ghost of pure glass, fingernails caressing the ice above her, sending soft, rippling echoes that she will never hear. Her body has known these waters for many years; coatings of ice protect her face from the cruel, wrinkled hands of time. Yet no coatings could ever protect her from the jagged hands of a million lightning bolts.

Clouds of thick, black smoke encompass the lagoon, gleaming a white flashing light of danger. Arrows of zinging electricity shoot down from the cauldron of darkness high above, each crooked bolt hungry for its next victim; yet the only victim available already had life sucked from their body. Thunder strokes dart all over the lagoon, destroying anything its merciless hands could find.

Isolation is replaced by chaos.

Fire streaks across the clean white hills, the artwork of sky replaced with a deadly, bleeding purple. Forks of electricity unite together, forming a globular ball of power, heat; life. The lightning hurtles down from the lethal source above, breaking the sheen blanket of illuminating ice, freeing the dark depths below.

Freeing the dead girl below, as a million lightning bolts strike her directly in the heart.

Silence. Then…

A breath…

(Middle) Antarctica. Perilous, threatening, isolated. Never in all my career have I recorded a lightning storm this extreme in such an icy, dry region. The blazing orange of our dingy glinted off the sparkling ice, cracked and shattered as a result of a cruel bolt. Burned, black hills surround a destroyed, isolated lagoon. Murky purple and black cover the vast sky above us; electricity has zapped the beauty out of this place.

I have not been equipped with the best of teams – they all seem to be very junior in their knowledge of meteorology; compared to me, anyway. I was assigned as leader of this expedition, as it is rather clear to the company that I am the best at what—

"Oi, Jenkins!"

The sound of a rowdy, South London accent irritably interrupts my train of thought. Turning around to address the noise, I raise my eyebrows, acknowledging him by the bare minimum.

Seemingly distraught, he raises a quivering finger to point at the wrecked lagoon ahead of us. Revolving back to my previous position, I see nothing to my interest.

"What is it, son? Never seen a hill before?" I remark, smirking. "You see, to a mind as dim as yours, a hill could be presented as something…"

"Damien," this time a more respectful, sharp voice, "seriously. Look down there."

A breeze, chilling and darkening enough to seep through the layers of my large jacket, gusts around the lagoon as my eyes scan to a sheen blanket of illuminating ice, which was damaged most by the storm.

But what I see next is more chilling and darkening than any breeze; a girl.

No, a ghost.

Hair as dark as a raven's wing, dripping with what could have been mistaken as blood. Frost covers her intricate, vintage wedding dress. Burning blue eyes, lips, skin, bore into mine, as she impossibly, managed to heave her convulsing body out of the dark depths below.

She was the definition of death's door step.

Eyes glazed and swimming with fear, her mouth trembles violently; she seems to be trying to communicate.

"H-h-h-help." My ears can just make out her weak voice.

My team is sitting here, traumatized, no-one able to function. She becomes hysterical at our blank response.

"Help! Help me, I plead!" Her voice wails, with a Brazilian accent. "I want your help! I am death." She starts sobbing, helplessly. "I am death... HELP!"

Respectable Voice clears his throat, swallows hard.

"Damien?" he whispers, hoarsely, "What should we do?"

"Nothing," says Rowdy Accent, "d-d-don't let her on the boat. Whatever you do, please, don't–"

Common sense chucked aside, I pull at the motor, zipping across the water towards the girl. Rowdy Accent wails, terrified of the danger ahead of us.

Reaching over, I wrench the scorching cold girl onto the

dingy. Wrapping her in layers of blankets, remembering my first aid.

"Miss, it's okay, I'm here to help," I reassure her, trying to rid her of this panicked state. "Stay calm. I just need to ask you some questions to check your health, okay?"

She nods, narrowly understanding my English.

"Can you tell me your name?"

"Adriana."

"Good. And can you tell me what year it is?"

This seems like a harder one. Her face contorts into a struggling expression, thinking hard. Coughing and spluttering, the answer finally reaches her: "1897."

"Miss, the year is 1997. Surely you must know that?" I ask, now becoming the struggling one.

She stares at me vacantly. "The year is 1897."

DEATH'S CHANGE

BEN MALLIA, YEAR 9

*N*o. No is the word I hear repeated from Eli, my new step-dad. My mum adores him to the point he rarely gets up from the greasy, stained, cheap sofa we have. Unless he needs to 'show' my mum what she is to him by punching her. She often has a black eye. I want to say something but I'm usually locked in my cramped room struggling to think how my mum is holding up out there. Every time I hear anything, even myself, I scurry to cover, which is usually my mattress. The fear fills within me and I get taken into the deep black abyss of pain and suffering where I feel most at ease as I know I can't be touched by anything apart from abuse from my own mind.

I quivered as the deep croaky voice of Eli entered my mind. As this happened, I was snapping back to reality or hell, there's no difference to me. I soon after crumbled down to my damp old floor and gathered up any stray thoughts and embraced myself for the torture-like beating I was about to receive.

It felt as if I was just a stress ball to him and my sole purpose was for me to let him relieve stress from himself and make him happier. After it happened, I shuddered and ran to cry in my bed.

I cry but it hurts. I soon rise with a creak and crawl over to a mirror to a site I never wanted to witness. He gave me a black eye. I refused to overcome the fact I can do anything. But my mental state was in such critical condition I couldn't even imagine how my mother was feeling. But I was interrupted by a creak of a door.

I hid under my bed until the recognisable face of my Zac, my brother. I asked him what was he doing here. He replied with a cry-like moan. I requested again to know why he's here.

"I'm here for you and Mum."

I was confused to what he meant by that. So, I asked what he meant by that.

He said, "Eli is in hospital."

I lit up then shut down. Finally, Finally I'm free. I began to whimper like a hungry neglected dog as all the memories dashed through my mind and into the mental fire I now believed in. I sprung up but I heard a voice. It sounded like Eli but I ignored it. Then Zac vocalised the words why are you happy. The following words were so bad it was like a spear just entered my heart. They were, "Chris that's my GIRL-

FRIEND!!!" I turned white with pain, fear and most of all guilt. The feeling my brother was expressing had to be disappointment.

Then he did something strange. I was concerned so I ran over to his side to come to a site. There was a pool of blood! Warm, thick oozing blood. As I kneeled down to his side I held his sweaty, soft hands and witnessed him take his last breath and soon following with his head lay back. Lifeless. My whole body shuddered and then soon I realised it wasn't a suicide or accident. It was a murder! I look deep into his blurry lifeless pupils and at that moment I realised that it was Eli I was looking at. At the next moment I was fleeing into the kitchen. I was soon confronted by a shadowed figure. Hood down and in their left hand a bloody, runny stained butcher knife. I studied the body as a scientist studies an atom. I soon recognised I've seen this body before. It was family. That's when the figure pulls back their blackened hood to reveal a face I never thought I would see. It was Zac! At that point we both knew we had to disappear from the face of this disgusting, painful, wrenched, ruined, tainted world we truly despised.

THUD

LAUREN MCINTYRE, YEAR 9

"Aus! Stef auf, geh raus!"

*E*ven the solid, surrounding wooden walls of our cabin quiver and rattle ever so slightly with the banging of fists that could only belong to soldiers. I attempt to prise my eyelids apart, fused together it seems with thick, gunky sleep. The loud banging continues, rattling my brain to the point that it genuinely hurts. Bang! Bang! Bang! They're coming. Through the slits in my eyes, I see a few other men slumped together in a defensive huddle in the centre of the room. More are emerging from the wooden wracks they call our beds; all wearing the same torn, filthy striped garbs they call our clothes. As always, I stare and watch the same, familiar cycle of hope leaving their sunken faces, as they go from contentment to confusion, realization to misery. They are not back home. Nor are they safe, nor are they happy. They are not rocking in an armchair, nor are they cosied with a book. They are not playing piano, nor toasting in a pub. They do not play, they do not laugh, they do not smile. As for these simple pleasures, it seems a man can only dream.

Bang! Bang! Bang!

They're coming. I have watched countless men die, countless men beaten. Bloody, raw, bruised. Starved, shot. And I have learned from every single one of these. I suppose, these things I have seen, have taught me the lessons that the beaters of the beaten, and the murderers of the murdered, wanted to teach me. They have taught me what not to do. One of those many lessons, perhaps the most vital of all, was never to draw attention. Ever.

I must get up. Currently, I am the only one still to refuse to face the daily trauma that has become my life, hugging my knees, squeezing my eyes tight shut as if they were gates to reality. Today, I will see more men die. Today, I will see more men beaten. I shall see men cry and scream in agony. Today, I know I could easily become one of them. Refusing to accept this now just makes that more likely.

Just as I have managed to drag my stiff, aching body to the rather vulnerable outer edge of the huddle, the door to our hut swings open with such force I think it has knocked several people over, who find themselves being violently pulled upright by multiple arms dressed in thick, immaculate green fabric sleeves. The cabin has erupted with mass panic and confusion, and before I can even get my bearings, we are being herded out like sheep onto the muddy field outside.

We are out in the open; it is still dark out. But the soldiers are marching us forward in a jumbled line, and despite not being able to see a thing ahead of me for the heavy fog and the older men, most of which are double my height, I sense the familiar route to our work station. My body is bashing hard against elbows on elbows, throwing me left to right, left to right. We've finished the straight path now, and I autopilot turn left onto the road that leads to out to our station. But I'm wrong, because as I turn left I run into a soldier's club that throws me the other direction. Before long I've found myself in and unfamiliar building. Its interior resembles a changing room of sorts. I am momentarily in a state of utter confusion, not understanding a word of the foreign commands being barked at me.

I start to see people undressing and, without thinking, I find myself doing the same. I stand there fully naked, trying hard to ignore the fact that I could count every rib. Then we begin to move once more. I'm tripping over legs as I attempt to follow the crowd that seemed to be heading for a small door at the end of the room. I'm shaking, I've made it through the door and am now wedged hard between other withered bodies. It all happens so quickly. It goes dark. The lights go out. I can't see a thing. People are screaming, begging for help. The pleads rattle my ears. Silently, I join them, praying in my head with more passion and fear than ever before in my life. That's when I hear men collapsing around me. Thud! Thud! Thud! I try to scream but nothing comes out. Air is refusing to enter my lungs. I'm fighting to stay alive, but it's as if I feel my organs are giving up the battle, accepting defeat. Perhaps I'm ready too. I close my eyes one last time, squeeze them tight, and wait for my turn to thud.

Thud.

.

FINALLY LOVED

GRACE MITCHELL, YEAR 9

"*E*sther," the soft shrill of Matron's voice echoing up the corridor was not a good sign, especially if it was accompanied by Matron herself.

Laura Bell was the matron here at the orphanage and even though she cared deeply for the children in her care she couldn't help striding around with an air of self-importance following her everywhere she went. "You're supposed to be getting ready!" Her words were firm but sweet and no girl ever thought to defy them.

"Ready for what? Rejection? Again!" The brave backchat sass that came out of Esther's mouth was a feat no girl who had ever attended Miss Bell's Academy for Orphaned Girls had ever accomplished. But with the rude response came a smile upon Matron's face. "You never know, we've got a lot of families here today," she responded with a smile, knowing immediately what

Esther was talking about. Matron knew why this day was tough on this girl in particular, and that she needed to be very tender and patient with her. "They're all the same," Matron sighed. This girl would try anything not to attend adoption day! "Come now, Esther there may be someone, now go, shoo," Matron tried one last time with an air of sympathy. Esther finally gave in and dragged herself up the old musty wooden stairs to her dorm.

As Esther sat in front of the chipped, spotted mirror in her room, beds crammed together reserved for other children her age if they came and weren't taken straight away, like they always were, she thought staring at the brown paint peeling of the walls, that were well past they're refurbishment date. She leant down and heaved up a loose floorboard, whose nail had fallen out.

Underneath was a golden locket in the shape of a heart with an 'E' carved out in the middle with little flowers tied around it. Her parents had given it to her for her 6th birthday. As well as the locket, there were letters from her parents sent to her during the war, and an old worn leather diary, which she had been writing in since her parents had died when she was seven.

They had died in an unfortunate bombing during WW2 in the middle of Liverpool. No one had told her until she had come back from her foster home in Cornwall, the news was broken, and she was whisked away here. They had all been very sympathetic and gave her the space she needed but as time wore on, they grew more aggravated in finding her a home away from the orphanage so she could be happier and loved properly with a family of her own.

However, the fear of being abandoned, betrayed even left her rejected and hesitant which took its heavy toll and she grew to learn she would be forever unloved.

Esther finished brushing the soft wavy locks of her blonde hair and, setting the hairbrush down, she began to cry. Clear pearly tears rolled down her perfectly porcelain cheeks and emitted a soft splashing sound when they hit the plush white pillow case on her bed. She realised the truth: she would remain here to rot forever, unloved with no friends but her diary.

As she buttoned the back of her dress, it fell to her knees in a soft cascade of velvety purple, she braided her hair, buckled her shoes, clasped the locket around her neck and grabbed her diary, slamming the door shut behind her.

The couples were taking their rounds looking at each girl individually. Esther sat in a corner with her diary, listening to the echo of footsteps draw close and draw away. No one wanted her, no one ever had, and no one ever would. She sat there in a puddle of despair and sorrow, minding her own business when, Matron came up behind her and whispered softly in Esther's ear, "There's someone here to see you." Her breath hitched and she spun around hope glistening in her eye.

One hour later, Esther was waiting outside Matron's office, hands clasped together in hope. And as the clock chimed five she squealed in happiness as adoption papers were signed and it was Esther's last night in the orphanage. As she sat on her bed in the moonlight with her diary open and pen in hand, she wrote:

Dear Diary,

The impossible happened today. The day I never thought would come, came. A couple came and spotted me in the corner. Once they saw me, they asked to see me, they asked questions and looked me over, I loved them straight away and they loved me back!

Papers have been signed and they pick me up at eight.

I can't believe I'm saying this, but I finally feel loved.

Esther xxx

FOR VALA

ELEANOR DANIELS, YEAR 9

*J*ake jumped, backpack falling with him. Concrete rushed towards him as he rolled, breaking his fall. 10:50p.m. his watch declared: ten minutes to disappear before the estate's owners came back.

Quietly, quickly, he bolted from the Manor. The darkness swallowed him up, making him no more than a shadow. His heartbeat slowed as more distance was put between him and the scene of his crime.

He had just dropped to a walk when suddenly he heard a sarcastic voice behind him. "That was a good run Jake!"

Jake spun around, cautiously waiting for any sign of movement. The voice's owner walked casually out of the shadows – a lanky teenager with hands in pockets.

"I, Jake, am from VALA and my Director has a proposal for

you." Without giving Jake any time to think the stranger rushed and put a cloth over his mouth. Jake blacked out.

Cluttered and chaotic was the room Jake woke up in a compact office that looked as if a paper grenade had just exploded. A bog-standard desk stood in the middle with battery lamps on it.

Jake found himself slumped in a plain wooden chair facing the desk. Behind it, seated, was a young woman about sixteen years old.

"Finally!" she said, with a calm you knew couldn't be good, and looked straight at him.

Jake squinted at her in the dim light. She had pale skin, bags under her eyes, nails painted dark red. On one, the paint had flaked and was shorter and more jagged, not that any of them were incredibly long. Her hair was carrot orange, or maybe slightly darker, and pulled into a tight bun. Even with the sereneness of her features and distressed appearance she was mesmerising.

"My name is Raven, Executive Head of VALA. I have a proposition for you."

"VALA? The ones trying lower the voting age?" Jake snorted.

"Yes. That's the reason why the Voting Age Liberation Association *was* started. Our plans have… developed."

"So why am I here?" He paused… "Developed?"

"You may or may not have noticed the country is in complete

disarray. And whether you care or not, this is going to affect everyone's future and under 18s don't even have a say in it!"

Jake groaned.

She gave him a withering stare. "I'm not asking for your opinion. I'm asking you to listen to my proposition." She continued…

"Our plan is to drive the Government into utter chaos. They've done the most part for us already with their ridiculous referendum. Now we need to make it absolutely clear to the British public that the Government is utterly incompetent." She smiled with a slight vicious edge to it. "Then we will present ourselves as a sensible, alternative option to the chaos. We'll show younger generations can bring equality and unity to the Nation."

"How does this involve me?" Jake asked cautiously

"As a notorious thief, we need you to break into the Houses of Parliament with some of our specialised hackers… so they can implement our new technology"

"Technology?"

"Let's just say that our science department has created a fingerprint scanning device that looks identical to the one that's part of the security for MPs as they go into the Houses of Parliament."

"And what does your scanner do exactly?" Jake was intrigued.

"The scanner releases a microscopic 'smart' dust which

dissolves into the finger and communicates to us. It allows us to control the MPs' minds. We'll be able to make sure they don't agree on anything – chaos will flourish."

"Sounds very exciting and everything, but I never do something for nothing." Jake stood up, despite having no idea where he was going.

"We will pay you substantially," she said calmly, standing too.

He turned to face her and looked down to stare her in the eye – she must really be quite short because she was wearing heels.

"One-thousand pounds plus sanctuary should you ever find yourself in need of somewhere to lie low."

"Two-thousand."

"Fifteen-hundred."

"Fifteen-hundred and I'd consider it but I would need time to construct a plan."

"If only we'd thought of that!" she spat! "Look Jake, we have a plan. We just need you to put it into action. Follow me. The crew will show you how everything works."

With that, she walked out of the room. Her demeanour signalled she expected him to follow.

Two hours later, back in Raven's office, Jake's mind was buzzing with everything he'd witnessed. A group of incredible, intellectual teenagers had showed him a plan which seemed both unbelievable and extremely logical. Their hacking technologies and devices were from another dimension.

And yet they needed him to get them in. It was so dangerous and on a scale he'd never attempted before.

"So," Raven interrupted his thoughts. "What's your decision?"

Jake considered the plans again in his mind. His heart raced.

Then slowly a smile started to form on his lips.

THE GHOSTS OF GRIEF LAKE

MADELEINE DAVIES, YEAR 9

*I*s life grief's magnet? If so, does an end to life bring an end to grief?

Thoughts jostled for attention in the crowded cage of her mind. Mel's limbs flailed as she stumbled over grassy hillocks in her desperation to reach the pier. The icy water beckoned; filled her with an overwhelming urgency which surely only the water could quench.

At last she reached the lake – an endless expanse like a field of rippling lead. Identical to the mouth that had swallowed her parents. Gazing into the bottomless depths, Mel squinted. An image had appeared.

She watched, transfixed, as the raft was pulled further into the abyss. Though the child laughed, the image looked tainted as if viewed through a lens of sadness. Or truth.

Attached to the raft was a quaint boat, tugging the raft with a grim obstinacy. A haze of happiness clouded the child's vision and she laughed unabashedly. Rays of sunlight glinted off the golden watch on her father's wrist.

Without warning, the boat gave a sudden lurch, flinging her parents into the welcoming water. Helpless, Mel called from the raft to the gasping figures writhing in the lake. This was no time for hesitation: she dived headfirst and let the ice engulf her, wrapping its fingers around her freezing body in a fist.

Forcing her eyes open, Mel searched frantically for a hand in the murky darkness. Muffled voices cried out in terror and she opened her mouth to answer – to reassure them she was coming to save them.

Still on the pier, Mel watched herself struggle. Bubbles emerged to the surface as the air was crushed from her lungs.

Slowly, the image faded and Mel was left staring at her own reflection. Tears ran down pale cheeks, though it could have been lake water.

Around her, the temperature dropped and a cloud clawed across the sky to block the Sun. A faint breeze chilled Mel's bones and she turned to face her fears.

Outlined against the trees were two translucent apparitions. Frail, as if the breeze would blow them away. Water dripped from their clothes and on the wrist of the man was a golden watch, the hands eternally frozen at his time of death. They glided towards Mel, floating a mere inch off the frosty ground. Anger flooded from them.

Lies.

Their words crept into her mind, resonating with appalling dissonance. She clutched her head and let out a piercing shriek. The truth had to stay locked away.

Yet nothing could be done. Mel screamed; another image appeared on the lake's surface. In a hysterical attempt to escape, she lunged forwards only to be snatched back by tendrils of smoke: the dead have power over the grieving. Control of her body was lost and she surrendered to the reality.

The same scene. Lake. Boat. Raft. Family.

Without warning, the boat gave a sudden lurch, flinging her parents into the welcoming water. Helpless, Mel called from the raft to the gasping figures writhing in the lake. This was no time for hesitation. But she did.

Mel watched them. Watched them while they drowned.

The memories hit her with full force, knocking her breath away and, for a second, it felt like she was drowning.

Now you feel what we felt.

Sobbing in anguish, Mel unlocked the door in her mind that had been shut since their death. Truth and grief are incessantly intertwined. Life and grief come hand in hand – detaining truth had brought back to life what grief sought. This took Mel to the question. Does an end to life bring an end to grief?

Coldness swept across her. The ghosts tore through her body

and dragged her, pleading for forgiveness, to what was destined to be her resting place. A final scream followed by bellowing silence.

~

"Such a shame what happened to her – poor gal. They say she went mad after her parents' deaths."

"What happened?"

"Both of them drowned. Then, a few weeks later, her body turns up in a lake. Suicide probably."

"I heard they found her father's wristwatch on her. Proper strange, that."

"Don't seem strange to me."

"The watch were buried with her father."

'GUILTY'

MARTHA TIZARD, YEAR 9

"Your Honour, the members of this jury find the defendant… guilty."

I watch as Isher's heart rate increases as his fellow colleagues sigh in relief.

"This court is adjourned." The Judge stands up to leave and gives Isher a knowledgeable smile as he glides past him.

"All rise," the Bailiff says, and Isher stands up, straightening the creases in his suit. He always was a smart man. He then reaches over to shake the opposition's hand. I watch as Isher looks at the culprit. The man he has condemned to a life in prison. Yet there is still a smile in the offenders wicked face. This man won't see his family for the rest of his life, and he isn't showing any signs of remorse in the slightest. Not even one tear is shed. This is when I can tell Isher knows this man is guilty. It is solidified when he spits at Isher, leading him to aggressively wipe it off. Never the type to tolerate rudeness. In his own opinion, All Isher did was help him on the journey he needed to get his life back together. The man in cuffs ruined his life for himself when he decided to push that lady off the bridge and into the water. He is an 'unlawful' murderer. I think he's a hero.

As Isher walks out of the court room, I take in the differences of everybody's characters. It's not like anyone has drastically changed physically, but mentally everyone acts is as if they have swapped life with another person. They remind me of me. The way they are one way somewhere, and another some-where else. The Judge is hugging his young son. Moments ago, he was locking a man up for the rest of his life. The Bailiff, who seemed so happy in the court room, leaves and his smile is replaced with a sad looking mope. For him, work is his life. And now the case is over he will have to go back to normality until he is asked to help solve a case again.

Then you look at the cleaner going into the room and clearing up all the leftover drinks and food. He's going to get paid in four hours what Isher spent last night at dinner, even worse is that that is on the main course alone. He is doing more work then I probably ever will and gets payed an abysmal amount. In a way, I feel sorry for him. But then I remember, maybe it's his fault he is where he is. Maybe he didn't listen or pay atten-tion in class, and then he didn't get the grades. Then he wouldn't have gotten into a good college and then he would have had to get a bad job. Maybe, if he had listened in class, he would have done better in tests, and his grades would have improved. Then he would have been accepted into a good college and then maybe a good uni and before you know it, he could be where Isher is now. One small change, even one as small as listening in a lesson, that makes a huge difference.

You see, Isher doesn't notice change. Not like I do. I could walk into his life a completely new person and he would be none the wiser. But in this case, I don't mind. Because I need to get back into his life. Thanks to him, I've changed. But he won't notice, and that's a good thing. He still trusts me. He still thinks I'm the innocent twenty-year-old I was. He is my key to freedom.

Yes, I've killed a man. And Isher knows. So that only means one thing. Isher must be next. I've been watching him for weeks and have come to a conclusion: it's me, or him.

HERO

MAYA CLOWES, YEAR 9

$\mathcal{M}$y head started to throb and beat intensely. Sharp pains occurred every few seconds. A wave of dizziness hit me and I went from standing to collapsed on the floor. Before that, it was a perfectly normal day. I woke up fine. I got dressed fine. I went to school fine until right before lunch when it suddenly hit me. Once I was on the floor, all I could hear were faint noises and sirens in the distance.

I woke up in a bed, about a day and a bit later. I first assumed that I was in a hospital as I had just collapsed but to me it looked unusually dark for a hospital. I sat up quickly to see a figure sitting in the corner of the room in a large chair, but I could not see their face. The thing that freaked me out the most was that I could hear what they were thinking. From what I could hear, I managed to find out that we were in a top-secret base and there were two guards standing right outside the room. Apparently, I was 'powerful maybe even dangerous', which was intriguing. The figure got up as if he was aware of what I was doing and slowly walked to the end of the small, dull bed. Eventually, I could see his face as the light from the small window hit him. I never quite got his name, but he explained everything and told me I could trust him. He explained that my powers had been triggered causing me to collapse. They had been watching me because they knew I had powers but only now they had surfaced, had I reached my full potential. He offered me training as I could be an asset to their team, and I would actually be known as a real super hero. I was speechless once and I knew I could trust him because I could read his mind. Everything that happened to him everything that he believed in and he could never keep a secret from me. No one could.

Over weeks of training, I had realised I could do more than just read minds: I could control them. This is why they thought I could be a danger because that power is a great responsibility. I was powerful, I have never felt powerful before. My life had changed and there was no hiding from that change.

I was walking back from a hectic day of school of trying as hard as I could to control my powers and not accidently read someone's thoughts or tell someone to do something they don't want to do. It was really sunny meaning me and my best friend Lucy, who goes to a different school, were going to the pier to go on the rides. I was now walking down Lakeshore Drive when I heard a squeal coming from a small alley way right ahead of me. My heart began to pound quicker as I slowly walked forward and peered down the dark alley. There was a tall man holding a gun to a young and smaller man's face who was shaking and on the brink of crying as he was being yelled at for his wallet and watch. I didn't know what to do but then I realised. I didn't need to call the police or yell for help I could help him myself. I took a deep breath and I remembered all the advice I had been given over the past month on how to use my powers I stepped in front of the alley and stared directly at the man holding the gun.

"Put the gun down!" I yelled as loud as I could. The man slowly put the gun on the floor.

"Kick it towards me."

The man continued to obey my every word.

"Now, on the ground there until the police come. Do you understand?" I said firmly. The man muttered, "Yes," so, I picked up the phone and dialled the police. Once I got off the phone and looked up again, I saw the look on the face of the man I just saved who seemed amazed that a small girl like me told a huge man what to do and saved his life. It was at that moment that I realised I could make a difference and I was a real super hero.

HIDE AND SEEK

JASMIN GOHARRIZ, YEAR 7

*U*nlike the others, who were living in hell, we had escaped that from the beginning. Although we were always in constant fear, it was better than the rest. Since it all started, we had been living (all five of us) in the attic above my auntie's house. If she got caught, she too would have got prosecuted. It was a game of hide and seek, but between life and death.

It was small, but enough for us. We were just grateful to be here. It was risky, but our only choice. It was scary, but our path to life. The room was very limited and there was nothing to do, however we couldn't do anything about it. Blacked out windows, mattresses on the floor. I liked to think it was a trampoline park. Fun for a while, but it got boring very soon! No carpet, not even downstairs, we rarely ever went downstairs! It wasn't safe; if anyone came to the door we would have been one of those people on the trains. Going to a place of horror.

At first, I didn't really know what was going on. It was complete loneliness. No one to play with. No one to talk to. Then it all got worse. I remember waving away to dad as he pulled his rusty suitcase onto the train. We never heard from him since. It was now just the five of us fighting for survival. Without much help, we survived the first six years before they started searching for us. Thousands must have been found but yet again, we were safe. I know most had either fled to safety, others grouped onto trains by the thousands

Sounds of gunshots filled the air, smells of dead and destroyed empty buildings. Trains were leaving constantly, packed full, like herds of cows in a field. Only later would I know, that those same people would never return! The hatred for us was unreal. Not like others, although I could never work out why. It had been like it since I was young!

In the distance (so far away) clouds of smoke flew out of the large pillar. Every morning, every evening. It carried on for miles up into the atmosphere, creating a blanket over the city's buildings. Something about it stroked fear. The sky darkened into a faint violet.

Begging every day, I wanted to go and make some friends outside on the streets. That would never happen. The yellow star we were meant to wear would have revealed to everyone our secret identity. It was like spies but not fun at all, only imaginary games we could play. It wasn't like all the other 'normal' kids; we were trapped in a 4x4m room with nothing to do, nothing to see, and barely anyone to talk to. Life was a misery, we never knew when we were going to end it all, neither did many other people in the country. Many had by no choice every day!

It was that day there was a knock on the door. A vigorous knock. Knocking like you have never heard before. An urgent knock, it seemed serious so we kept silent. Not letting anyone know where we were in hiding. I heard it. The one thing I had been hoping not to hear for what seemed like my whole life! There was nothing to do. It was over, the nightmares that appeared in my dreams every night had come to life.

They were here, here to search for us. Stamping up the stairs like a herd of elephants, opening every door they saw. Silence, for at least a minute before they tried to get up to the place we used to call safe. This game of hide and seek was now over!

HIGH RISK CHANGE

GEORGE SIMMS, YEAR 9

*A*s the roaring wind rushed pass my slender face, it made me wonder if what I was doing was worth it. I had been travelling for many days and it hasn't been easy. I have little to no food. My entire body is sun burned to a crisp. My feet are covered in sore blisters. The only thing keeping me going is the hope that I can get to a safe place. I heard there are camps in countries to the far West who help immigrants like me. I have been following this long road for days now, with no idea where it will lead me. A couple of cars have driven past me, none of them giving a damn about me. But maybe that's for the better. I decided to take a short break. I sat down on the cold ground and took a deep breath. Just as I let my guard down a blaring horn sounded behind me, followed by the gentle hiss of a truck slowing down.

It's been what feels like a day since I got in this truck and I'm not sure it was the greatest of ideas. I mean sure, I'm moving much faster than before. But I'm sitting here, hungry, surrounded human waste. I am travelling with a couple of others, all from Syria I believe, but we haven't talked much. There are two children travelling with us, I can't believe that children are being forced to do this. From what I can gather the driver is going past one of the safe camps and he is going to drop us off there. I may be in a bad position, but what other choice do I have.

I don't know how long I've been in this truck. Hours? Days? Weeks? Every now and then the driver comes and gives us some bread and water. It's not much but we thank him for it. The truck has been stopped a couple of times, but they never find us. We're too well hidden. As the truck slowed to a stop for the millionth time it suddenly dawned on me how tired I was. I haven't slept a wink since I got on this truck. It's just way too uncomfortable. And that smell, its just impossible to sleep. Suddenly the back of the truck opened up to let the heavenly light seep in. In the gateway, the bulky silhouette of the driver gestured for us to come out. We had made it.

I let my eyes adjust to the light before I stepped out onto the hard road, I took a deep breath of fresh air. We finally made it. We're safe. My legs felt weak. My head hurt. My arms ached. But I have never felt better. We all thanked the driver then headed towards the camp. I was surprised by the normality of the camp. There are children playing football. There are people going on runs. There are even children learning in school. Yet they're all refugees like me.

We all headed deeper into the camp to see if we could find the leader. I saw how the people have used whatever they could find to build a community. They used scraps to build housed. There people farming for food. All of this was built from nothing, it's inspiring. As we walked we saw a building that looked like some sort of town hall. This was it. This is the building that will make us safe. Make us happy. Make us free.

IT'S ALWAYS THE KIDS' FAULT

JAMES WARD, YEAR 9

a single tear rolled down my cheek. My whole body was paralyzed and stiff. Those were the words that I dreaded the most. My parents told me they were getting a divorce.

Chris, my younger brother, was balling his eyes out. Dad shouted at him, "Man up!" I comforted Chris and put my arm round him. He was now sobbing silently, trying to hide his emotions from Dad. Mum was rather voiceless and didn't say much at all for some reason. She looked extremely pale and frightened, as if something bad would happen if she spoke. She just kept her eyes fixed on the floor. Everyone went to bed sad and depressed that night. I lied in my bed, just thinking, "Is it my fault?"

The next morning, I woke up to Mum and Dad arguing again, I think Dad hit Mum because she had a bruise under her eye when she gave me my breakfast. When I asked her, she said the same thing as last time: "I tripped." I think that the divorce was the first time she stood up to him, I'm proud of her.

At school, I just pretended that everything was fine; no one would understand, not my friends, not the teachers, I don't even feel comfortable talking to the P.E. teacher, Mr. Terry, and he's been really nice ever since I became the captain of the football and rugby team. I have a lot of friends at my school, they like me, I just like school in general, it takes my mind of things that happen at home. I get in trouble with teachers quite a bit, it's quite fun to be honest. They often phone Mum and Dad though which doesn't help. I'm very different at school.

It's only been a couple days since Mum and Dad announced that they are getting a divorce and things are already starting to move quite quickly; I saw Dad looking online on flats to buy as well as packing up a few of his things into boxes. I wish this could just slow down, I always knew that their marriage wasn't great, but I wish this never happened, it's a bit selfish of me to say but it's too much for me to handle.

On Saturday and Sunday, I work at my local coffee shop, I'm only fifteen so I can't get a better payed job but the other people who work with me there are actually very nice, especially this girl called Faith. She always listens to what I have to say and gives great advice, she's the only person (outside my family) that I feel like I can talk to about the situation at home between Mum and Dad. She's very special to me.

School this week was terrible. Chris told some of his friends about the divorce who then spread it around school. He then started to get bullied and picked on and they were saying how it's, "Probably his fault," and, "it's always the kid's fault," and they were also making fun of how he was wearing the same clothes to school every day even though our parents can't afford new clothes at the moment. I didn't know what to do. Every day he came home crying. This situation is so terrible.

Three weeks have gone by now and Dad has decided to move out and go to his parents' house whilst the deal for his new flat is being finalized. I really want to move out as well and start a new life of my own with Faith who I have now been 'seeing' for a couple weeks but I'm worried how Mum and Chris would survive. I don't know what to do.

LONG NOSES KILL

OSCAR DRAGE, YEAR 9

*W*hy?! *Why do I have to stick my God-damned nose into everything! Here I am in the middle of the woods at who-knows-what-time; my best friend's been blown to smithereens; and now I'm being hunted down by a dangerous syndicate who want nothing more than to kill me! Well done Kage! This is a huge mess, even for you!* I scream in my head before pummelling my skull on a tree.

After spending what seems like five minutes hammering my brains out, I stop to compose myself before resuming my attempt to knock out what little rationality I have left in my useless brain.

Ok! Now that I am thoroughly brain dead, I decide to stop and take a Crunchie from my rucksack. I receive great pleasure in peeling back the golden foil, revealing a rich cinder toffee bar laminated in silky chocolate. This small sense of normality helps me to regain a level head and stirs an appetite. I quickly speed through another three of these common treasures and a handful of purple baubbled grapes which I had hastily packed earlier. That's when I realised that the last time I ate was yesterday morning, when it happened…

It was Saturday morning and I had gone out early to treat myself to a Bacon and Egg McMuffin. I was on my way back home with smudges of ketchup in the corners of my lips when, suddenly, a sharp glint of red light caught my eye. It was coming from a dark alleyway beside me. The alleyway had grimy, dirt-smudged walls, splattered with obscenities, and the floor was covered in stinking bin bags. And yet, foolishly, curiosity got the better of me. I slowly waded through the bin bags, ignoring the stench penetrating my nostrils, until I could make out the object. The closer I got, the less glaring the red light was and I realised that the object was very small. It was a dark and very complex geometric shape with flat sides that I could only describe roughly as an x-shape. I had never seen anything like it! The light was unearthly, and the dark grey material looked like it was light but incredibly strong. That was when I spotted the source of the worst smell in that alleyway. To the left of the strange object, in a dark puddle of blood lay a grotesque sight: a severed hand!

I cried out in horror, tripping over and scrabbling frantically among the sea of bin bags, trying to get up. When I got to my feet, I sprinted out of the alleyway, spraying bits of egg and bacon which add a fresh coating of vomit to the already splatted wall. All of a sudden, I noticed a sharp pain cutting into my palm. Looking down I saw the mysterious x-shaped object embedded deep into my flesh, causing black spots that clouded my vision. Eyes wide with the fear of the horrific outcome, I ran back towards the safety of my apartment where I could call someone about my urgent situation.

My hand shook manically as I tried to force the key into the small lock, triggering me to yell foul words at the door, eventually collapsing into the apartment. I assumed my flat mate and best friend Jay was still at work, so I was going to ring him to tell him that I needed his help but then the phone started to ring. I was so desperate to talk to someone- anyone, and I practically dived for the phone.

"Hello Kage," a menacing voice harshly cut in. The voice was deep and robotic, the accent unplaceable. "We know who you are, we know where you live, and we know you have something that belongs to us." My throat constricted, leaving me unable to speak and shaking even more. "Something embedded in your hand!" the voice growled aggressively.

That was before it resulted in the blowing up of my apartment, turning my friend into a pile of ash for good measure!

"So here I am in these God-forsaken woods, having the worst day of my life. I've lost my sanity, I have no one to turn to, and it has been absolutely..." I froze instantly. The cold muzzle of a gun was pressed firmly into the side of my head. "We tried to warn you, Kage. It didn't have to end like this," taunted the deep robotic voice. "But your actions to try and evade us only sealed your fate!" At this line, I forced myself to look up at the gunman and what I saw, I could never have anticipated. There stood my Father whom I had thought dead before I was born.

"Didn't anyone ever tell you, Kage?" he mocked, "LONG NOSES KILL!"

LOST

MAYA PATEL YEAR 9

*E*veryday is a new me.

Everyday I feel as though my soul doesn't belong to me.

Everyday is as confusing as the next and the next and the next.

Everyday is a new me… but I'm not.

A wall is the only thing that divides me from her, both physically and psychologically. Just the thought of her presence haunts me. I don't know when she'll return, I don't know how long she'll stay, and I don't know when she'll leave.

What scares me the most is that I know what's happening to me yet there's nothing I can do about it. Multiple personality disorder: yes, it's as daunting as it sounds.

It was five years ago when I was diagnosed. The day remains

crystal clear in my mind, but I wish it didn't. It was an average day for a twelve year old, however I woke up feeling different, not knowing she had taken full control of my brain. I remember the pure agony of having to listen to this stranger, who I couldn't control, in the back of my head. Just imagine someone is in possession of your thoughts, forcing you to think the way they do, but there's nothing you can do to stop it – you can't fight it. All you can do is wait. Wait until you regain control. That's how I felt whenever she came.

Useless. Helpless. Trapped.

You would think that I got used to her, but every time was as surprising as the previous. It felt as if every time was the first, however over the years it began to become more bearable. At the start she would come once or twice a day, then it increased to five times a day. Minimum time spent one minute, maximum, four hours. Having two personalities, especially for a twelve year old, wasn't normal, but I never stopped to think how distressed my parents felt about my condition.

It was three years ago when he came. I was only fourteen at the time of his appearance, and as you can probably imagine for a young teenager of this age, he was by far the scariest of them all. He was the complete opposite of me, thereby making it more difficult for me. He was a nightmare.

Every night I would pray that he wouldn't take over me.

Sometimes it worked, sometimes it didn't, because when he came was when I was in the most pain.

What made his presence so unbearable was how he didn't just control my mind; he controlled all of me. When she was in control, I had some management, however he overtook me, leaving me imprisoned in my own body.

There was a day when he came that I can remember distinctly. I was walking home from the school and I bumped into one of my classmates. I don't know how it happened but it felt as if our encounter awoke him. He suddenly got really aggravated and out of the blues he just started yelling at this poor kid and there I was just sitting in the back of my head as if I had front row seats for a drama. I was screaming and pleading to be set free, yet there was silence. Even my own brain wasn't listening to me. I couldn't have felt more neglected. Little did I know that that was the last time I'd see him.

Five years ago I was a completely different person to who I am now. It used to be just her, him and me.

Now, I wake up with a new pair of eyes everyday.

Everyday is like following a map, but without any signposts. For an ordinary teenager you wake up with the same emotions, the same views and the same pair of eyes to which you see the world with, so finding your way is quite straightforward. But for me it's difficult. I wake up not knowing what personality has entered my consciousness. Without my identity, I'm lost.

Ever since he left, I have been able to block out any of those that I don't want in me. Some I decide to keep, but some I permanently discard.

I am no longer afraid, weak or powerless. I am confident, strong and powerful. My personalities are my compass, without them I wouldn't feel complete yet with them I will find my way.

Everyday is me, and I am in control.

MAGIC

LILY HOBBS, YEAR 9

*M*y pocket-sized friend lay limp on the ground, his cotton stuffing scattered like daisies. Stitching was loose, leaving the button eyes lifeless. Pulsing not far from me was an aura I knew too well.

"Sorry it had to come to this, kid. Really, I am. You were good, so, so very good to me, but I'm gonna have to let you light that candle now."

Realisation rushed through me as I realised what he meant. How could I have been so stupid? I had been played.

The trees around us swayed as the dancing fire pulsed another beat, causing the flora to resemble an old movie. Contrasting to how it looked when we started this journey.

"You set this up?"

His lips curl at the sides.

"You don't have to learn magic to be considered smart, Heather. I've helped you before, all I ask is for you to return it."

Instead of creaking again, the wood underneath my feet snapped in half. My screams replaced all other sounds as I frantically tried to find my surroundings. Heather coloured strands of hair blocked my view as I fell deeper and deeper down into the ravine. Closing in on me, the knife-like edges of the wall seemed to get closer every time I looked at them, driving fear further and further into my pounding heart and scrambled mind, forcing me to wish for something, anything, to change this fate. And then... everything was still. Heart still racing and breathing uneven, my eyes met with a pair of buttons. Luci was holding onto my hand with one of his, the other was occupied with the rope from the bridge.

Something wet trickles down my face and I notice that I was crying. With the rope tightly in my grip, we slither our way back up to the surface. Small droplets of water hit my hand as I place myself on the grass, Luci dabs them away with his fabric. It was that moment that made me rethink everything.

"Everyone probably thinks I'm dead, why did I ever think I could do this? Maybe you should have let me hit the floor instead of saving me, everybody would be spared the disappointment."

I could see their faces as if it was happening again.

"We won't burn, we won't hang, and we won't let them try to drown us. Peak, that is where the protection will come from,

I'll cast a protection spell." Their eyes are screaming, "It's a hoax," but hope is also there.

"Take this, to protect you." Placed in my hands is a pocket-sized cotton doll with button eyes. My protection for the climb ahead of me. Standing at the foot, looking up, I place my hope that it is at the peak. "Hey, Kid. Let go of me I can fly without help you know." Something squirms in my grasp, I look down and see a pair of buttons.

"Name's Lucille." He had an edge to him, something almost... demonic.

"Looks like it's just you and me, Kid." Little did I did I know, the blabbering wouldn't stop; apparently it doesn't matter whether a doll's mouth is stitched on, as long as there is possession. Lucille had a big mouth for someone so small in size.

"I swear to you, if your mouth wasn't already stitched... I knew I should have brought that black candle." Soft chuckles echoed off the trees around us. "No matter how many candles you light, my friend, I won't leave you alone." With his stitching already in a smug grin, he had the audacity to taunt me further.

Tears brimming in my eyes, I look up to be met with a pair of blue eyes plastered to an emotionless face.

"Lucille?" The name barely rolled off my tongue. His height meets mine as he floats down from where his spirit took a human form. "Wiccan, not a demon. My spell was almost complete before they came, all I needed to do is to light a candle. Or should I say...need." Outstretched in front of me was his hand, my bag contained all of my items, so I gave him the handle. "You have every right to hate me. But I did consider you a friend. I am truly sorry." Not a single word can escape my lips before I find myself where I started only a few days ago. At the foot of the mountain, on the outskirts of my hometown.

MY BOOTS SQUELCH IN THE MUD

JAMES GARNER, YEAR 9

*M*y boots squelch in the mud. The black cinder streets are so eerie in the early hours of the morning. Few people are up but the occasional swarm of miners pass me, motionless expression on their sunken faces. The light sound of their tin buckets held in their blistered hands and swollen knuckles breaks the deadly silence.

I reach my parents' rundown shack on the outskirts of the village. The door is half open and on its last hinge. I take a step inside, crouching so I don't hit my head on the low ceiling. There is only one cramped room in the shack, not uncommon in the slums of the village, but it's icy cold. The manure and hay walls don't protect the occupants from the blistering cold air. The smell hits me, it's the smell of vomit, blood, puss and mucus. My eyes scan the room until they land on a woman wrapped in blankets. I slowly pick my way across the room to where the victim lay, anxious not to alarm them any more than I have to. Placing my bag of herbs down, I open it revealing hundreds of small glass jars all with a different herb inside and a label identifying it.

"Hello," I gently whisper. "I'm here to help"

A hand emerges from the blanket, it's missing fingers and is deformed, covered in tiny cuts. I try not to gag as a face emerges. Haggard and withered, but not with age, it resembles a brain. Her jaw is deformed, she has no teeth. But her eyes, they reflect the deadly charcoal clouds that spit down their ferocious acid rain. Their beauty losing to the plague that consumes her and saps the life from her dying body.

Suddenly, we are no longer in her shack, we're now in my home ten years ago when I was still being trained. It was calm and peaceful but when I look down at my patient she is gone and my own mother takes her place. Her face is deformed and she has no teeth, her face is wrinkled. The look of desperation in my mother's eyes is the same look that haunts me to this day. And then my younger self enters the room, she looks too innocent and pure to see such horrors. She is carrying my mother's herb bag and places it down by my mother. She must have forgotten something and runs out the room to grab it. My mother starts coughing up blood. I don't know what to do, my heart races and tears roll down my cheeks. I panic and try make a cup off anti-cough tea but my hand just glides through the jars. Breaking down in tears, I beg for my younger self to return. When the coughing abruptly stops, I freeze, my heart misses a beat because I know it's too late.

The room once more becomes dark and cold, a foul smell

filling my nasal cavity. I am back in the shack. I turn around realising I was never gone, to see my patient motionless. I check her pulse, nothing. Then it dawns on me, I could have saved her, it was my fault.

After covering the body, I leave for home, my boots squelching in the mud, the charcoal clouds looming over me. I think about the old lady and my mother, how she looked after me and cared for me on her own. I think about how my life changed when she died, taking her job so I could eat and drink… and I'm grateful.

NOISE

MOLLY CHATWIN, YEAR 9

*N*oise. All I can hear is the deafening noise of my new neighbours across the road. Four nights in a row. 2:53a.m. on the dot, never a minute later. I throw on my dressing gown and slippers and march down the road planning to confront them. I start pounding on their door with all my might, but the music is filling the air blocking out any other sounds. I don't give up but the low-pitched music (if you can call it that) is starting to turn my brain into mush. I walk home holding my head in my hands trying to think straight but I need some well-deserved sleep to do that.

I've been sitting in my bed with the pillow over my ears for hours moaning and yelling thinking that it might do something to help but nothing. Until 5:30a.m. when I heard it. The blissful silence. I heard nothing. Not even the birds were awake. They were asleep in a flash. Similarly to me. Before I knew It, I was asleep, dreaming of beautiful hills and graceful sunsets imagining I was there just lying in the long grass. It was heavenly but it was short lasting as the walls of my dreams where being penetrated by what sounded like a soft fire alarm which meant I had to get out of bed and get ready for work.

After my paper round I treated my self to coffee when I bumped into our local electrician. We got to talking and he told me about his eventful weekend with his granddaughter.

He said, "She had found the electric box and cut all of the power in the house as a prank. Kids these days, am I right?"

I just nodded and rushed of as his story had given the perfect plan. There will be no music if there is no electricity. It was perfect. I stayed up all night to think this through. When my alarm went that meant it was time for the first stage of my plan.

The first stage was waiting till all five of the neighbours had left the house. No matter how long it would take I was going to wait for all of them to leave. I have packed up all my equipment in a bag and I am ready to leave. I am in my bedroom window staring through a pair of dusty binoculars and I see it. The last neighbour had left. Stage two was ready for action.

The next stage was getting in the house. I have done hours and hours of research on how to pick a lock. I practised on my bathroom door and I have gotten very good at it. I sneak out of my house and I'm standing, frozen at the front door wondering to myself should I be doing this, but then I remember all the restless nights they have caused me, and I glance into my bag I retrieve everything I need, and I see the back up equipment. The back up equipment is some of my building stuff. It will take of the door completely. Anyway, I go in. I am twisting, turning and pushing but I can't seem to open the door. I don't understand. I have been so good at picking locks. How come I can't pick my dumb neighbours' door? Then it hits me. They are not smart enough to lock their door so I burst in, excited and mischievous, and sneak down to the cellar with my equipment ready for the final stage.

The final stage was the easiest. All I needed to do was swap some wires so that there would be no power. Well there would be some power so that they are not suspicious, they will just think their ridiculous speakers were broken. I switched the wires and got out of their house, and not a minute to soon because a few of them where returning from where ever they were.

I get into bed and hope and pray that the speakers will not work. I fall asleep and I dream that same dream again. Magical fields and warming sunsets with me slap bang in the middle of the field, just relaxing and enjoying the sunsets. That is until a wall of sound is launched right into my ears, turning my dreams into dust. I roll over and switch of my alarm. Yes. My alarm. I have never been so happy to wake up to it. My plan had worked. I had succeeded and I had a glorious night's sleep. And I will for the rest of my life.

NORMAL

CAL DARRAGH, YEAR 9

The house was cold, a lingering layer of false security glazed over the town as a sharp wind awoke the pristine man who was neatly tucked into a bed. Frozen azure eyes shot open to scan their surroundings. The man took a short, controlled, yet exasperated breath as he looked into the small closet, to only be disappointed with unfolded undersized clothes. Stroking back his calmly parted blonde hair, fashioned with tamed beauty, he made his way down the frosty stairs tightly gripping his wife's pale hand.

"How many sugars, darling?" he spoke with ice seemingly resting in his throat.

Silence.

"A little shy this morning?"

Silence.

Treading over crystal shards of broken glass, the man of poised stature started to make his coffee. Coffee, hot water, milk but no sugar.

"Where do you keep the sugar, darling?"

Silence.

"Ah here it is, thank you." But as soon as the process began it was ruined; by the corner of his eye he spotted a grain of sugar hiding on the work top. Violently he hurled away everything, cup, coffee, sugar and milk. The process started again but successfully this time, and the coffee was formed in pure perfection. Still gripping his wife's hand, they made their way to the oak table making sure not to scrape the chair on the icy floor.

"This reminds me of how we met, darling."

The day was a bright cheerful Tuesday at 3:46, the sun was skipping around the town smothering the darkness with new light. He spotted her in a lazy coffee shop sitting alone, her brown hair shining in the sun, reading one of his favourite books: 'Wuthering Heights'. Her eyes stole his gaze with their unique beauty, her rosy, lively skin inviting his attention.

"This seat taken?" He spoke with an odd surge of charisma.

"Now it is." She winked, inviting him to the seat. They talked for hours and she was perfect, kind, warm, beautiful but best of all.... alone. The conversation of strangers became a memory of lovers as they talked until the shop closed its homely doors. He placed his icy hand on her soft, precious hand and lovingly swooned back to her place.

～

His train of thought was interrupted by a loud knocking at the door, the knocking was irritating and reckless, so it had to have been a child. The man cautiously opened the door, engaging the safety chain, but he was correct; in front of him nervously stood a scrawny boy no older than 14, his blonde hair swept across his tanned face like a wave of gold. Pathetically he tried to form a sentence whilst being crushed by the raw pressure radiating from the tall man. "Le..etter for... for Miss Darling?"

"She doesn't occupy this house anymore."

"She was here yesterday though." "Run home…"

Surprised and somewhat terrified, the boy ran away still clutching the letter. He paused at the end of the driveway, concealing himself behind the dirty bins, and waited.

As the night drew in, and the pale moon glanced over the frosty town, the two newfound lovers found warmth and comfort in the young girl's grand house. in a flurry of passion, romance discovered the two enjoying their time together with flirtatious displays of affection. His piercing eyes locked with hers whilst their bodies danced until the beautiful silence was broken by her soft, precious voice. "I think I love you." Silence.

. . .

Slice.

Abruptly she stumbled back clutching at the small, neat blade in her throat. She lost her footing, crashing into a glass vase and shattering it. Warm drips of sticky crimson liquid flew from her, covering the man. Her hands grasped at the wound in panicked distress only birthing new blood to drench him. He simply stood there, no expression, then he spoke.

"I never introduced myself. My name is Antonio Smith. I'm an only child. I work as an architect in this small town. I enjoy the simple things – walks, coffee, books and the stimulation I get from taking the lives of pretty girls such as you, my new, wonderful wife."

Gripping her hand and rising from the freezing table they began to wander out the door, stepping over the glass, past the coffee and through the door. It was quite picturesque, the sight of the man clutching a singular pale hand and walking away to freedom

ONE ORANGE, TWO GREEN

ROSIE RELPH, YEAR 9

The yellow ones with milk, the pink with water. Billy's mum was extremely fussy about her pills. One orange, two green. GOALLL!! Billy's favourite team had just won the World Cup in the last few seconds. No. One orange, two green. A life paused. Again. Billy urgently wanted to watch but he knew mum was more important. Shuffling slowly up the narrow staircase, Billy glanced quickly at the dusty, cracked picture frame that sat all alone on the window sill and, all at once, the sick feeling in Billy's stomach came flooding back. The sound of sirens, the crunching of metal, the stench of petrol lingering around him. Billy had to sit down. His hands were uncontrollably shaking. Breathe and smile. There was always the same empty space next to his mum, where his dad used to lie, and the same rainbow of pills. He pulled up his mum's shaking body and lightly patted her head with a cool flannel.

"Oy Billy, did you watch the big game last night?"

Billy hastily shook his head. "Got other cool things to do." Smile.

As Billy carelessly chucked his Chelsea backpack into his locker, he caught a glimpse of the girl he really liked. Violet. Her eyes were bright blue; her hair was silky and golden. Just like Mum's. Billy loved the buzz of school, he loved all the attention, and he loved it when girls giggled as they walked past him and his friends. He always looked forward to fifth period on a Friday afternoon because he had Maths. Mr Raduman was his favourite teacher, he made Billy feel the same warm feeling he'd always felt before the accident. He made him feel clever. He made him feel normal. Suddenly, the bell rang and the realisation that the day had ended hit him hard.

Billy always dragged out the walk home; it was the time when he could think. It was the time when he could think about Dad and the accident. It was the day before Dad's birthday. 14th June 2006. Mum was laughing to Dad's awful singing as Billy danced along in the back. The warm hum of the radio was suddenly cut short as Mum's scream sliced through the air. Silence. The first thing Billy could hear again was the glitching of the radio and the piercing screams of ambulances and police cars. The stench of petrol lingered around Billy's nose as thick, dark blood seeped slowly out of his shaking leg. The bright blue lights of the ambulance beamed in his eyes as an impulse of emotions rushed through his startled body. Dad was gone. He could feel his absence. Billy had just experienced the scariest ten seconds of his life.

The yellow ones with milk, the pink with water. Billy's mum was extremely fussy about her pills. One orange, two green.

PANGEA AND THE GREAT SAMURAI WAR

LEO MACK, YEAR 8

Leo Mack, 8GC

Long, long ago in an ancient land called Pangea there was a Great War: The Great Samurai War. And, as usual, it was caused by greed and the wanton need for power.

The domain was ruled by four Samurai Lords: Lord Lite; Lord Angus; Lord Anne; and Lord Venom. They were wrestling against each other to become Lord Regent, 'RULER OF ALL'. One of them stood out among the others being unkind, cruel, vicious and spiteful: Lord Venom, leader of 'The Venom Order', and he was indeed very E.V.I.L (Evil, Villain, Iniquitous, and Loathsome).

The War had been a long and bloody affair, with the victor being E.V.I.L Lord Venom, his brutish army had eventually with the use of their sharp, blooded curved swords, overcome, slaughtered and vanquished his rival Samurai Lords.

For five years Pangea and it's people suffered under E.V.I.L Lord Venom's reign, but one thundery night, unbeknownst to all asleep, a mysterious blood-red cloud appeared floating over the battlefields of The Great Samurai War. As it traveled over the land, it gently rained a ghostly red mist across the bloody fields and where it fell there was a stirring and moaning, bodies were moving, slowly, digging their way out of the soil, picking up buried weapons and armour; the mist was resurrecting the slaughtered Lords and their soldiers, soldiers wanting revenge, revenge for their honour, revenge on the Venom Order.

Now resurrected but tired and weary from death and not battle ready, Lords Lite, Angus, and Anne joined forces against their common foe and secretly planned for revenge against E.V.I.L Lord Venom.

So, the BIG questions: As they had been dead for years, where was Lord Venom, where was he hiding? How to find him? And who to ask? How would they get fit? So, they started by asking their stunned and bewildered besieged townsfolk.

The townsfolk would tell them nothing, worrying for their lives as the Lords and soldiers were too weak to defeat the Venom Order, but promising wailing aloud, "We will tell you when the time is right. First you need to get yourselves fit by training extremely hard. Your training tasks are to build a pyramid for each individual army."

The Samurai Lords couldn't believe what they had just heard. "But it will take too long to complete," Lord Lite yelled, reluctantly. But he had to agree to the people's terms. Each Samurai

Lord in turn informed their own army – revenge would be sweet.

From block to block, day and night, the Samurai toiled hard on the pyramids as if their lives depended on it. One group would make the blocks of limestone, another group would pass them on to another group who would place them. Slowly but surely, the three pyramids were created from the bottom to the top, they were each a colossal 500ft high and when the sun shone their marble caps sparkled. In the end it was a great feat. Unbelievably, they had spent an astounding two years to finish them, but leaving all three armies fit and healthy and ready for war.

They honoured their promise, no longer worried the townsfolk finally divulged to Lord Lite, E.V.I.L Lord Venom's location high up in the snowy wastes.

"TIME FOR WAR."

It was time, next day the Samurai Lords and soldiers said their farewells to the village and townsfolk, and began their long and arduous journey through jungles, mountains and snow, finally arriving at The Venom Order's base, with an enormous army, battle ready, awaiting the three Lords and their Samurai.

Then, like the devil himself, a figure dressed in black armour arose from the hoard upon a monstrous black stallion with a look of confusion on his face. "HOW were the Samurai alive and healthy? They were dead seven years ago. Am I dreaming? Are you real? How is this possible?"

The Samurai answered together, "We are back from the dead and here for revenge!"

And the two armies clashed, colliding together, causing a deafening roar, swords clattering, soldiers screaming. Amongst the deafening noise, Lord Lite suddenly noticed there was something strange about this fight, that the samurai side had the upper hand and that The Venom Order was weaker and they were being killed much quicker.

"OH!" and E.V.I.L Lord Venom was standing on his own now having to fend for himself, he made a swift move to get away but Lord Lite was faster, grabbing a bow and arrow, three... two... one... the arrow went swift and straight, through the evil heart of E.V.I.L Lord Venom, leaving blood spewing out of his mouth and body, killing him instantly.

Now reigned by three Great Samurai Lords, Pangea was finally at peace.

PEOPLE LIKE ME

ANNABELLE SHAW, YEAR 7

People like me undergo pressure every moment of our existence. It stays with you for the rest of your life, hanging onto you like a scorpion with its prey. The sound of my unsteady and copious breathing was all I could hear for a while, until I made out pulsing footsteps only a few metres behind. I begged the ones above for them to just pass by; but of course, my luck had once more run out. Bracing myself for impact, I told myself to stay calm, don't get stressed, it'll all be fine. But the memories tormented me once more, laughing in my face and punching me in my already churning stomach. The palm of a stranger's hand had barely touched my shoulder before I spun round. All I noted after that was the screaming, the honking of car horns, and the repetitive thudding of me running away, away from everything.

Stertorous, sharp sirens and lustrous, blinking lights was all I could make out as I was pulled away, not understanding that this was the last time I would see clear daylight for a long, distant time.

Pattering rain on the cold, hard surface, thickets on either side (if you could call a mound of thin twigs and a few leaves thickets), it almost felt soothing, despite the whistling wind angrily whipping the sky like a rancorous circus master. Weird to think that if someone were to hit hard, it was likely to reduce to smithereens, piercing skin if that someone were to so much as brush it with an arm; yet, on a misty, dark day-like today- you could lean all body weight on it, and it would stand firmly in place, no matter how heavy that weight may be. It had been a day of injustice; it had been a day of cruel surprises; yet, it had started out as a day of normality.

Dew. Damp. Fog. These all seemed to mix and create a mildewy kind of smell, moving with the dancing air so one could feel it twirling, then going on to engulf the scene around, partnered with the unnerving silence- almost like people could tell what was to come: for the roads were empty; the nature was left undisturbed; there was no-one in sight. All except for the pattering rain on the cold, hard surface.

Four austere walls, surrounding you, as you try to see the good that could come out of this, or the hope that isn't there, again and again, until you feel so dizzy that you're reeling inside your mind, thoughts swirling as something would in a blender. Discomforting messages plastered the walls written by previous detainees: counting the days; cries for help; repeated words about what was being done. None of this helped my already shaken conscience, seeing that it was near to torture in there. I had been left alone, no company, no form of entertainment; just 4 walls and a window.

Those iron bars, constantly feeling like they're closing in, as you hunch up on the floor, getting smaller and smaller until it feels like you're not there at all. People fake it when they get out, acting like it's all sunshine and rainbows, when in fact, it's not, and it's eating you up inside. All that you see changes you, and most people never go back to their old ways, because they're petrified that if they return, they won't get a third chance. Still, I suppose it proves a point. That people can change. People like me. Maybe we can forgive and forget?

From Dad.

POPPIES

KENZO PATCH, YEAR 7

*O*nly the most eager and most dedicated mothers could nourish the keystone that resembles remembrance on this planet. The core reason of this being's existence is to show acknowledgment and beauty once it has fully matured into its final developed form. It rises from its age-long slumber – after what feels like years to some but months to many – thanks to nature combining its strengths to give it life. Its slender body structure pokes out of the dirt shriveled up like a prune as if it were squinting because of the sun beaming down upon it as if it were its father. Its two bird-like foliage wings make it stand out in the plain, drab, arid, open field that it stands alone in singled out as if it were a corpse in a crowd, only there was no crowd and it was on its own.

Many weeks later more it would transform, trans mutate even, into a more advanced mechanism of nature. It would grow legions and legions of leg like structures below the surface that would not only support it but also keep it hydrated. Its elegant foliage wings had multiplied and had grown making it look like a dragonfly taking flight, only with rugged wings that looked like they were maple leaves. But they were no use for these as they were held back, imprisoned, detained, a fish caught entangled in a fishing net, a fly in a spider's web.

The next modification to this asset: a carnivorous looking flesh-like burst of red incased in a green case with short black prickly static hairs covering its entirety of the luminescent colored capsule. Its entire frame looking like a Hydra with its nine heads, curled up ready to pounce at an unlucky victim. The green capsule reminiscent of a sea oyster with its raven black shell and fleshy center. Plenty of weeks later it prepares for a wedding, putting on a luxurious blooming red dress, flourishing, swaying in the wind as if it were dancing. The different hues of red like the difference of the sweetness and bitterness of an orange. Its center piece looks like a heart beating dangerously slowly but steadily pumping blood around to make the fabric like substance of the dress blood red. The red dresses display, like a piece of scrunched up paper in the dust bin but as if it were done on purpose to make it look even more unique, in its own way – as if it were a dog in clothes or cat riding a motor bike. The difference in the folds of the scrunched-up paper creating shadows on its self as if it were holding something in the way of the sun. A month later it would have to put away the lavish, elegant, clothing and change to a more basic every day state of clothing a piece that looks like an aqua marine colored t-shirt with the slightest specs of green scattered across the surface area encapsulating a peaceful calming aura around it. The outline around the nullified version of what was a once growing, developing part of nature has ran out of time and the clock will now stop for the legend that was this being and now it must spread its knowledge before shriveling up and fading away.

REMEMBERING

EMMA SHEPHERD, YEAR 7

rudging forwards over crunching leaves. Seeing them drape like gold medals round the fingers of a tree. They shimmer. Shining spotlights move in and out of the branches of a forest as tall as the Eiffel Tower. Whispering winds whistle around me.

Taking another step forward, the aroma hits like a bullet, the barbecue my dad used to make, before he left. Effulgent, bottomless oceans stretch out in front while standing surrounded by twisting, turning, tangled tree roots tying me down at attempts to drift away. Glass like dew covers the grass reflecting beams from an electric light out there in the universe, millions of miles from anyone. Like I am now. Miniature tornados cross the trodden footpath, the wind carrying tap-dancing leaves as they scuttle across the floor. Squirrels performing gymnastic routines, swinging from elaborate, luxuriant tails on the uneven of bars of nature. The air tasting sugar-coated like the brownies my mum would make, all those years ago. Sun shining like a blood orange. That was when I was last free.

Sadness spreads throughout at hearing knocking echoes from an antique tree, the sound of enclosed life. The leaves keep falling as they start to fall. Cascading like dominoes. Oceans begin to flood, the roots letting go but somehow pulling myself back. Nothing feels the same any more. Coal stretches across darkening skies as electric pulses of light push through. It crackles, snaps and comes tumbling down, pushed by darkness as light is destroyed. Trying to look round, there is nothing to look at as it drops to the ground everywhere. Nothing focusses (like when trying to take a photo), it just blurs into a grey haze. Blank canvasses, but I have nothing to paint. Water spreads like when something is spilt across a table; no choice but to push through, an Arctic forest that stretches before me. Nothingness stings like it did that time, when everything changed and I have scars to show for it. A bath tub overflowing high in the sky but still an enthusiastic shower pumps more and more and more. There is no way to retreat, only to drive forwards through the treacle feeling. Squelching noises come from the ground, the sodden ground like a wet bath mat. It starts hitting me but it doesn't bounce like a netball or a football, it sinks in like the insults from those bullies.

Suddenly coldness grows like ivy up everything, down everything. The rain that fell for years turns bleak and crispy; it clings like sand to bare feet. Breathing heavily, sugar-fine, glittering crystals scatter into a cloud like bubblegum. No scents can climb past a rigid, glacial barrier that blocks their way. Stinging pain down an endless throat as shimmering diamonds land on my tongue and melt like chocolate. Crunching under lions' paws: a noise like snapping wood; a noise like nails down a chalk board; and a noise like the kick of chillies. Diamond glaze turns spindly trees into an ice sculpture. Crunch. The vibration echoes through lumps of ice that could be attached to me, but I don't feel anything. Anything other than a stinging pain. Soaking and bitterly cold (cold as the Arctic Ocean) as I peer into an icy mirror on the floor, nothing looks back. A sharp stalactite of glass falls on the ground, it shatters into thousands of pieces. No more leaves cover the ground. Was that how it ended?

SAFE PASSAGE

ERIN GRUENBERG, YEAR 7

27 March 1939
Wien, Ten o'clock in the evening, Westbahnhof.

*T*ears raced to my chin, I held my mother close, would I ever see her again? Shudders of sadness swept over me. With only two minutes to spare I was going to give my mother all the love I could.

"I want you to know, Anna…" A great cry shook her. "I will always love you. You're my tiny star."

"I love you too, Mama, and I could never love anyone as much as you… I'll come for you, after the War!"

"Don't say such silly things, my love, concern yourself, not me." The clock chimed ten o'clock. Dread washed over me.

For the last time my mother's smooth, warm lips kissed me, then slowly and dejectedly she handed me Walter, my toy bear. Then I took my luggage and climbed into a cramped carriage with three other girls, who might be pleasant to play with if we weren't all so upset. The engine started rattling and the whistle wailed. I ran passionately to the window and called throughout the forest of children-grieving parents.

"Bye-bye Mama, I love you!"

"Bye-bye sweetheart," she called back. "I love you too!"

Suddenly, the long red train sped out of the station, on that cold rainy night. I waved vigorously until my arm hurt. Desolate and heart-hungry, I pulled my thick, sable plaits away from the window and sat on dust grey sheets.

Walter and I stared at each other for a while, dreaming of our past life, but there's only so much a bear can comfort you. I raised my eyes and saw the other girls, each having their own silent conversation with their toy dog, cat, and rag-doll. I felt sick, not because I was speeding along a bumpy railroad. I felt sick because I feared I would never again see my loving mother; compassionate father; handsome little cat, Adalbert or my simple, cosy home. It was all too much, I had to sleep! Miserably, I lifted those dust-grey sheets off my bed and crawled in, not sparing a thought for pyjamas. I curled up into an apple and drifted off to my world of dreams.

I was at the bottom of the ocean that night. Fish of despair glided by effortlessly. Drowning, I grasped for the surface

screaming bubbles of agony, but I could not, for I was trapped,
trapped by the Seaweed of Melancholy. Just above the surface
appeared a bright light and I had a curious feeling – as you do
in dreams – that this was all the joy and elation I so desper-
ately wanted clothed in a luminous ball of golden light.

Snap! I've been awoken. I am yet to reach the reason why, so
slowly I opened my eyes and yesterday came back with a
biting flash. My head throbbed as I fell back to Earth. A calm,
steady lady was waking us. She shot me a smile as she'd seen
I was awake.

"Have some oatmeal, dear."

"Th-thank you," I replied bluntly because I was too tired to
start a real conversation. Even if those oats were warm and
creamy, I could only taste the thunder storm of misery
screaming inside me.

And then sunlight flooded the carriage. I lifted my chin and
saw clusters of mountains watching our train slide by, silvery
white snow on their peaks, hiding the disappearing pearl-like
Gibbous Moon. Fir forests painted the mountains' ankles
malachite. A fresh spring breeze tickled my cheeks through an
open window and I smelt the pine forest exhale. My spirits
lifted as I heard children laughing in another carriage. I felt so
alive. I would be safe in England. With Walter, courage, and
hope by my side, I looked at the girl sitting opposite me and
smiled.

SIX FEET UNDER

HOLLY BANWELL, YEAR 8

"*A*nd breathe …" Firm hands press my heaving shoulders down. "In… Out…"

I breathe – in, out.

"Slow… ease back into it."

I try to relax but it's hard to get back into the rhythm. My ears finally pop, and my eyes with them, as the background chatter of the other swimmers finds my ringing ears. I start to hiccup, each jolt shaking my whole body, water trickling out my nose.

People are staring.

That's the last time I ever try this in a public pool, I silently vow to myself, glaring at Dan.

But looking menacing is hard when you are hiccupping violently.

"That," I manage to wheeze between gulps for air and killer hiccups, "Is the last time I ever come here."

Dan sighs, "I thought you might say that, you look pretty shaken up."

"I am."

"Shall we go?"

"Just a second."

"Alex! Are you sure that's a good ide…"

Dan's words are lost to me as I slip into the water.

Your average public pool will be suffocating in chlorine, faded tiles slowly giving in to mould and a few unnameable objects on the floor.

This is your average public pool.

The foul chemical taste of chlorine numbs my senses as I drift soundlessly beneath the surface. I take a deep breath, plunging down deeper, and run my hand along the floor.

I hiccup again, choking out an air bubble, and kick off of the floor, squinting as the light draws nearer.

It only takes a few minutes for my system to change this time – not so bad as last time.

I've always been like this, always preferred breathing water to air. Air is too thin, you can't feel it around you like water. I had thought it was normal, that everyone could do what I did.

Dan was the first one to realise I was different – to tell me it wasn't normal.

Normal people don't change, they can only breathe air.

The next morning is cold and fresh, and so is the sea. Dan dips his toe in and squeals – it's pretty freezing.

I slide in, feeling the transition in breathing and kicking out further into the sea. I am an amazing swimmer, rather obviously, so I swim far out until Dan is just a tiny figure in neon yellow trunks.

It's relaxing, but I'm annoyed, because a dinghy is bobbing around above me and they shouldn't be this far from shore.

I'm staring up at the thing, when a little girl leans over the edge. She catches my eye, jumps back, and a gust of wind tips the dinghy slightly. But it's enough.

My eyes grow wide – she isn't wearing a life jacket, there's no one else in the tiny boat.

I dart through the water. It's not calm anymore, it's frantic. Waves buffet me back, slowing me down as I swim towards the tiny, falling figure.

What can I do? She can only breathe air, and she'll have taken in too much water already.

I breathe water…

As soon as I reach her, I put my mouth to hers and suck the water from her limp body.

She's so heavy, so it takes nearly all my strength to push her onto the dinghy, and swim beneath it, pushing it closer to the shore – I'm faster underwater.

I can just about see flashing blue lights through the murk. I begin to swim for the surface, but something changes. I feel like I'm suffocating, being pulled down.

For the first time, I can't breathe.

Is it the salt water? How long I've been down?

My mind is cloudy. I can't see. My muscles cramp as I sink.

I've always preferred water to air. It'll be a change to breathe water forever.

THE BEST DAY OF MY LIFE

MATILDA BILLINGE, YEAR 8

*I*t's January 23rd – soon to be the best day of my life.

The waiting room is far too hot, almost suffocating, so I have to physically peel my thighs off of the sticky plastic chair as I stand to cross the room. It's miniscule. A tiny, cupboard-like space with green seats and a harsh white light overhead which buzzes like an angry hornet trapped in a jar. In the middle of the grubby lino floor is an even grubbier table, covered in stacks of magazines. I pick one at random and take it back to my seat. It's a fashion magazine. As I leaf through the pages of beaming models and celebs, I feel a glimmer of smugness. After today, maybe somebody else will pick it up and find a picture of me posing between the pages.

It's 11:00p.m. now, almost time. I'm sick with excitement and practically trembling with anticipation. However, something is nagging at me, sat like a rock in the pit of my stomach, this nervousness that won't go away, that voice saying that it's wrong, that it's dangerous, that I'm being stupid... that it could all go horribly wrong.

"Emily Green?" comes a husky voice, even though the waiting room is otherwise empty. "Right this way love, that's it, the surgeon's ready for yuh." And that's when I follow a stranger into the worst decision I have ever made.

I can barely move, only look around in revulsion. The walls are greasy and layered with filth, in one place splattered with something rusty red that I quickly banish from my mind. In the middle of the room there's a high table covered with a faded cloth. But I'm not looking at any of that. I'm looking at the steel desk next to it. I'm looking at what's on top. I'm no doctor, but even I could tell you that any of these instruments inside my body could do me some serious damage. Some deeply buried instinct at the back of my head is screaming at me to run, but it's too late, there's hot breath by my ear, a sharp prick in my arm, and I'm looking down, falling down...

I'm vaguely aware of something smashing, but all I can see are block colours, more like smudges really, smudges blending together into one huge blur, dark and fuzzy around the edges...

Darkness envelops me.

It's like dreaming but not. A jumble of images and emotions, all mashed together.

I think about summer five years ago, when my parents bought me my first phone. Soon my world was steeped in social media, a place full of perfect lives and beautiful people, a fleeting glimpse into another, better, reality.

I see the looks on my friends' faces when I told them about my idea, their horrified, enthralled expressions. Expressions that are growing brighter, and brighter, until they're practically glowing, radiating brilliantly, painful to look at. As they fade into a screen of blinding white light, I try to tear my seared eyes away. And I realise that my eyes are open.

Was I asleep? Why is it so bright? But I soon remember where I am. I snap up sharply, my eyes wide, all grogginess gone. The first thing I notice is how tight my face feels. The operation. I wrench my body off the bench and dash to the waiting room, pouncing on my bag and digging my phone out. I switch it to selfie cam, not daring to breathe. I don't recognise the person staring back at me. It's not me anymore.

THE CURE

SOPHIE MYERS YEAR 9

What makes you human? For some it would be our knowledge of how the world works. For others it is our way of communication. But many believe it is to feel emotion. That is what makes us human. But less than a year ago, after the War, a brilliant scientist created a cure for our humanity. That is because our emotions are weaknesses. Anger, love, guilt, sadness… they all hold us back from what we could achieve and distract us from the bigger picture. But the tests the scientist conducted were on other humans and these experiments were illegal. The cure was said to be destroyed but the 'damage' was already done. Thousands had taken the cure in an attempt to end the feelings of sorrow and sadness for their fallen ones in the War. I am one of the many who took the cure in a successful attempt to stop the pain and as such have been removed from my house and relocated like the others.

They came for me in a pitch-black van late at night to avoid any witnesses. There were four guards escorting me to the unit and had masks on to hide their identity. I had known it was only a matter of time before they came for me as they had already come for countless people who lived in my neighbourhood. I lost track of time, but it could not have been much longer that a couple of hours. The van pulled up outside of a tall plain building, void of any colour and lacking happiness or any emotion for that matter. I slowly approached the building but was violently shoved forward and told to walk faster by the tall guards who were either side of me to stop me escaping. Not that I would if I could because I had nowhere to go and I just didn't care anymore. There were two more guards waiting at the entrance to take me into the place I would be living for a long while and eventually most likely be forgotten. I entered the chilly building and our footsteps echoed down the bare hallways leading down into the building's lower levels. Deeper and deeper, through a labyrinth of tunnels. Pitiful flickering lights barely illuminated the dark corridor.

We finally stopped outside a small cell-like room that you might find in a prison with a rotted wooden bed and quiet squeaks, no doubt coming from many rats slowly withering away in this pathetic excuse for a room, having lost any hope of getting out into the world high above us. I was roughly shoved into my new 'home'. The knowledge that I would never get out would have scared me before, made me terrified even, but now I didn't have to go through that suffering I would if I still had my humanity. Our emotions are a weakness and they stop us from doing the things we want, out of fear or lack of confidence. People who were to afraid to speak up are now strong enough to make a stand and have their voices heard because they now don't have the nagging doubt that has held us all back at some point of our pitiful lives. There will be more justice in the world because people are not biased. With this train of thought, I knew I had done the right thing in slipping all that remained of the cure into the city-wide water supply. Soon humanity will be free of the curse that emotions inflict upon us. And humanity owes it all to scientist who had had enough of the unescapable grief of losing her family to the war. That scientist… is me.

THE FOSSIL

TOMOYA WALSH, YEAR 7

*O*rso grumbled as his boss emailed him at 7:00a.m. He was tired after a discovery at the dig site the day before. He opened his laptop and sent a message to his boss that he would be there as soon as possible. Sleepily, Orso changed and ate his usual bread and cocoa.

Orso Umman was a geologist who worked in a small dig site in Egypt. His best friend, his partner at work, was called Sean. Not too long ago, the people working there had found a new species of animal. Scientists were trying to figure out what it could be but so far, no one knew what it was.

That day, when Orso arrived at the dig site, Sean was already there waiting for him. He had a broad smile on his face and rushed over to see Orso as soon as he saw him. Sean said that they were going to try an experiment on the fossil that had been found. When Orso asked what the experiment was, Sean gestured for him to see for himself so Orso went into the main tent to see his boss and the scientists.

On entering the tent, he could see that his boss and the head scientist had their heads together and were discussing something. Orso patiently waited for them to finish before speaking, eager to ask what the experiment was and how it would work. His boss replied that the scientists had managed to get a DNA sample from a scale which was attached to one of the bones of the creature. He explained that the scientists could use the DNA sample and the intact skeleton of the creature to create a clone of it, therefore bringing it back to life to learn more about its species.

Orso was very excited to start the process of bringing it back to life – he would be one of the first people to ever see the new species of animal in real life!

Later that day, when Orso and Sean re-entered the tent, the machine was already ready and was humming slightly. It was crowded by scientists who were working on the controls. Orso and Sean walked around it once and then took one of the seats each. Orso's feet were tingling with excitement. He and Sean were about to witness a miracle of science. The scientists turned on the machine.

Orso could feel the vibrations in his seat and the hot air in his sweat-covered face. The machine started emitting hot steam and was forming a shape inside the glass container. First, it looked like blob. Next, it looked like a cone. Then, it started to sprout things that could have been legs or arms. After that, it grew some wings. This all happened so quickly that Orso's eyes started to hurt but he didn't want to miss anything so he forced them open. Finally, the machine started to cool down and it stopped vibrating. All seemed eerily quiet.

The head scientist opened the top of the machine and stated that the creature didn't seem to have survived. Orso was a little disappointed but was glad that they could see it in the flesh. The head scientist started to pull out the creature when it suddenly spread its wings and screeched an ear-splitting scream. Everyone covered their ears and raced for the exit. It started to fly aimlessly around the room, or so it appeared.

When most of the people had left the tent, the creature settled down on one of the chairs and looked around, turning its head sharply. Orso had stayed behind to examine its behaviour and attitude towards humans. When he approached it, it stared at him for a full ten seconds. It reared up and spat something shiny out onto the floor. It was a sword. When Orso had seen what it was, the creature started to glow and shrink at the same time until it became a glowing ball. The glowing ball moved towards the sword and when it hit the metal, it disappeared. On the hilt of the sword, engraved into it, were the words 'The Sword of Awesomeness'.

THE INHERITANCE

ISABELLE CURREY, YEAR 9

*T*hese keys are so old I doubt they will even open the door. I jam them in to the small key hole, half expecting someone to greet me at the door. No one will though.

The first step onto the hard hallway floors. The cream paper lantern flickering. Coats were still hanging there on the coat stand. I slowly walk forward into the lounge. I see three large leather sofas with floral cushions. The cushions still had the imprint of someone who sat there. A brown coffee table sat in front with three half eaten cookies and a cup of cold tea lying on top. The sight gave me chills. I carried on walking into the kitchen. Clothes were laying in the washing machine with the red light still flickering saying it was done. The dishwasher was hanging partly open, with the fridge buzzing beside it. The kitchen sink was full of dirty dishes. Mainly cups.

I had come to this house once before when I was ten. My

uncle used to drink at least three cups of tea a day, so when I used to come into the kitchen dirty cups of tea would lie everywhere, so there was no surprise when I walked in the kitchen. Where cups laid everywhere.

My uncle and I weren't really close, I mean I only met him once when we came and stayed for a while, but I enjoyed the stay. I liked sleeping in the bunkbeds. I still have the teddy bear somewhere. He gave it to me when I came because I was scared to sleep upstairs. That was his fault however as he let me watch a vampire horror film called 'Fright Night'. It was a long time ago though, so I don't really remember the details.

As I look around the house that hasn't changed in almost 20 years, I find a photo of me and Uncle Jerry in the corner of the 'bunkbed room'. The chequered sheets and the old grungy carpet. I tear up and clutch the photo in my hand. His whole life sitting in front of me, was overwhelming to face.

I walk down the stairs, photo in hand and open the front door. "Come in," I say to the real-estate agent waiting outside. "Whatever price you think is best." I take one more look at the property slopped on the payment. It was time to go. I stoop into the car and take a deep breath. I jam in my keys and start the engine. Then I drive away.

I don't want that property; I don't want to live here in this cold grey drizzly country. I wish to stay in New Zealand where it rains in Winter and is sunny in Summer. So Uncle Jerry's house goes.

I stepped out of the car onto the curb. Tears of guilt filled my eyes as the vague memories of the week we stayed up at his house were coming back. I opened the hard wooden doors with the red tulips in hand. I place them down onto the cream covered table and walk down the corridor. The stone walls are intimidating. I take a seat by myself at the back on a long bench. Someone is just reading the end of a poem. "The stars are not wanted now: put out everyone; pack up the moon and dismantle the sun; pour away the oceans and sweep up the wood. For nothing now can ever come to any good." I knew the poem. It was called 'Stop All The Clocks' by W.H.Auden.

The speeches have finished and it is time to say goodbye. I walk back to the cream covered table and pick up the red tulips. Then I walk over to the wooden box. There I see Uncle jerry with his peaceful face lying there. He was holding a tea mug in his hands. I lay down the flowers and wipe away a small tear. This would be the last time I see him.

THE JOURNEY

MAGGIE PATMORE, YEAR 8

A flash. A whirr and a click. Blurry then focused. Vivid streaks of colour. Dull light streaming in from an open window, flapping curtains frozen still. Hospital sheets pulled close to the pale face of a young woman with a halo of shining hair, smiling gently. Cradled in her arms, her blue eyes meet emerald green in a silent welcoming to this world. Her child is gazing up at her with an open fist reached out in a gesture of trust.

Years pass and the same child is now set upon a pair of upright chubby toddler legs, dabbing swirls and splodges of bright paint on a messy canvas, hands splayed to create a handprint of ocean blue. Her future creativity was easily portrayed in her innocent features.

Bright sunshine and a group of smiling teens, one with a head of red hair, another with deep dimples and a young girl, rays of light highlighting their eyes. A spread of lush grass splattered with dewdrops blankets the surface of the park, sky lighting up in a blue flame.

Layers of stormy black swarming around a large community. Heads topped with odd square hats and dark cloaks pulled together in a joyous still image of people laughing, crying, and glinting with happiness. Bold letters strung upon thin string that flutters and stops in the gentle breeze stating 'GRADUA-TION DAY'.

White planks piled in a horizontal wall with a black slated roof blurred in the background of a towering sign, a girl leaning on its thick wooden pole. Beside her, a man, frozen in time, caressing her hair as it blows in the wind, strays flying from a trail of hair hanging over her shoulder. Large boxes stacked with an explosion of items for their new home to keep.

Ribbons of pastel confetti fluttering in the air, stuck as gravity and lenses fought a battle of stillness. A happy couple, dressed in radiant shades of white and grey, surrounded by waves of guests who had come to support them on their special day.

Another hospital, another mother, another child born into the world. Happiness radiating like bolts of light flooding the room with a warm feeling of calmness.

A large cardboard box, filled to the brim with various office supplies and a letter with the word 'Fired', a common use of pain printed on the sheet. Staff passing by – their faces, although blurred in the background, show obvious distaste

The hospital again but a different ward: one that retaliates sorrow, one where strange substances are implanted into the arms of a man. A woman and child stationed beside him, their shoulders sagging at every word the doctor reviews of the cancer patient, a constant frown disfiguring his face.

A church. An audience. A coffin.

Courtroom floorboards creaking under the weight of a teenage boy, glancing back at his mother, tears in his eyes signalling his regret. A judge seated before him, calculating the punishment given for numerous thefts at the age of 15. A car outside ready to transport him to another place, another area away from his home.

A living room, scattered with newspapers and old toys, empty apart from a middle-aged woman collapsed in an armchair. A rocking chair, an absence with it from where her husband should have been, and a padded sofa, where her son used to lie and read.

All empty. All gone.

A different view, outside on a grassy hill, and no longer an image caught in a split second of motion but a video. Several frames of silence.

"I can't do this anymore."

In the corner of the screen creeps a hint of a face, pale in the hurt of her losses, tears streaming from emerald green eyes, the same ones that first opened to see the world many years ago. The frame blurs.

"I can't."

The view drops with a sickening lurch. Glass smashes. Silence, and never-ending darkness.

THE NEW SICILY

SOFIA COSGROVE, YEAR 8

I walked past the desolate abodes, the jagged shards of gravel engraved themselves into my worn feet. Gunshots over and over like a broken record. They filled my ears. The blood-boiling Sicilian sun blazed down. This would be the closest near-death experience for me.

I threw myself from shadow to shadow, sticking as close to the crumpled piles of debris as possible. They were all over the country, crawling and multiplying like bacteria. The Mafia – merciless, cruel, and holders of bountiful amounts of money. At times I wonder about my opinion that they will eventually take over the country.

Shooting briskly towards a vacated cattle shed, I seat myself behind a vandalised half broken wall and breathe soundlessly, not wanting to be heard. You know those moments when everything goes silent and then one single footstep or breathe breaks the air? This is this moment. They study every detail of the auburn headed girl standing before them. Without hesitation, I lift pepper spray from my threadbare pocket and before making my well thought out escape, I blanket the cartel members' eyes in the vile substance. I would later find out that this was a major fault that would cost me. The borders had been closed early that morning, so no one was getting in or out of this warzone of power and wealth. You either kill or get killed and I'm not going like this. If my life ever comes on the line I want to know I'd die among the world's legends. I thought I was getting further away, safer. Little did I know, I was getting more lost by the second.

Sometimes people do things wrong subconsciously. It's all part of human nature, but it can be irritating at times, especially when you have to escape I'm guessing ten to twenty-thousand hazardous drug traffickers in the space of 9,927 square miles of land. Sicily was once a luxurious holiday destination. How times change...

THE SEARCH FOR A STAR

VIOLET ISAACS, YEAR 7

" *R*ight, next! "

As Hamilton began the audition process, he had a feeling that something was not right; no one seemed to be his star, no one in the whole of London. As each red/blonde/dark-haired girl came through and as each small or tall woman came out, he still could not find the right person. Time was ticking and in a matter of days, he would have his poster up outside the theatre saying the name of the star. But now there was no star and no star meant no play which meant the end of his career.

Last year, Hamilton had produced the best play out there. It had hit the five stars and sent people out of the theatre with ecstatic faces, winning him a clutch of awards. It made the public far and wide have a day to remember and a memory to keep. But the best part about it was he made some great friends and lots of stories to tell.

Each audition went by and when the clock reached 5:00p.m. and the last aspiring actress had left, he packed up his brief case full of head shots and forms and began to walk home. Although London was a big place, he liked the view of the river, the tall buildings and the hustle and bustle. Most importantly, it got him thinking what his future held and how he ever going to find his star.

The next day, Hamilton woke up to the knowledge that he only had two more days of auditions left, which meant he had to find a lead either today or tomorrow.

He got up and helped himself to a large coffee; if anything was going to help him it had to be his coffee. He read the newspaper and switched on the radio just to listen to the news and see if he had missed anything the day before. Although he had got home earlier then usual, he still had dark bags underneath his eyes and the same headache that has been there for the last two weeks.

At 8:30a.m. he set off only to find he was not the first one there. His assistant Gregg sat at the table his pale face looking whiter then usual and his hair not as neat as it usually was. Hamilton knew that he was thinking the same thing as him, although it was too late to ask. The first audition was a young girl with dark brown eyes, immediately Hamilton knew that was not the look he was looking for, so she was scooted out in a matter of minutes.

As time went by, each hour the same as the day before, he still had not found his star. He was anxious now and petrified that he would not find the right person. As he began to pack up his papers, he heard a voice from the corridor, it was so beautiful it almost was like she was singing. Hamilton had to find this delicate sweet voice, so he headed out of the room, only to find a cleaning lady! She had the look he was looking for, the height he had been searching for and most importantly she had the voice. There was a question though, could she act?

The moment she started to speak the words from the script, the character that Hamilton had written came to life. There was no question that his search had ended and that a star had been born.

THE STORM

DILLAN TURNER, YEAR 9

ightning cracked down somewhere nearby, perhaps the cornfields. Jenny, my sister, was in the living room somewhere. I peeked out of the kitchen window just as another bolt of lightning collided with Earth, no more than 100 meters away. Rain was seeping in through every crack possible. It was beginning to puddle up. The thunder was deafening and flashes of lightning constantly could be seen echoing around the wall of the farmhouse. It was a miracle that we hadn't been struck yet. Then, immediately after thinking that, a bolt of lightning caved in the wooden support beams of the roof.

The rain was flooding in, now about a foot deep. "Dexter!" shouts Jenny. I trudge through the water to find my sister; she was standing on the table to keep out of the water. I pull her in to my arms and waded through the water and debris to the door. I see Jenny shout something but I can make out what she is say because the thunder never ceases. We need to get to the city; it's the only way to find shelter. Just as I leave the house, a blast of light hits the stable ahead of us, a different one strikes the ground close to us. This was a mistake. I pulled her in close as another bolt hits the earth not ten meters away, another so close to us I could feel the force of the light. It was only a matter of time before…

WHAM.

Me and jenny were sent flying.

I remember a time when storms weren't as massive. I remember a time when ducking under tables and chairs to be protected from the earthquake wasn't a normal thing. I remember when I used to go to play basketball. When mother was alive. But the year is 2058. The time of storms that last days. The time of lightning strong enough to wipe out a skyscraper. The time of earthquakes strong enough to flatten cities. The time of death.

I woke to the sound of crying. I tried to stand but found I couldn't move. I tried to wiggle my finger and my toes. Neither moved. I look around but everything was a blur. It was like I was looking into the reflection of quickly moving water. I tried to say something but it came out as a blur. An obscure shape came above my head. It could be a face. I blacked out before I could make out more details.

I woke up again but this time it was different. I was propped up against a tree and I could see. My sister was picking away at an apple that looked actual vomit.

She looked up and saw that I was awake. "Dexter! Oh thank god! I thought you were dead!" she said with a sigh of relief.

"Wait, how long have I been asleep?" I asked bewildered.

"Four days"

"Crap. How are the animals?"

"We had a couple of cows alive but I don't know what to feed them, so… ummm"

"Don't worry about it."

"What are we gonna do?"

"We need to find Uncle Jack."

"But he lives in the city"

"And that's where we're going"

I stood up to look around and see where we were: the forest at the back of our farm. I walked through the trees to find the farm. I knew something was wrong as soon as I stepped out of the densely arrange trees. There were two large SUVs parked outside the wreck that was my house. I counted five, two waiting outside the cars one I saw poking round the demolished pig-sty. I've heard of this type of crooks, they would scour the ruins, looking to steal any valuables from the helpless victims left behind from the storm. Usually with violence.

I grabbed Jenny and pulled her back into the trees. We need to get to the slaughter house. We have an old lever-action rifle used to slaughter the pigs, which is in the storage shed. Fortunately, that was just a couple meters to our left, out of the forest. I dashed to get to the door, telling my sister to stay behind a tree, and fumbled with the lock. Finally, I burst in and scrambled to grab the gun from the shelf. I stood in the doorway and took aim at the guy siting by the tree. I breathed in. and pulled the trigger. He fell to the floor. The other one who was standing near the cars dived on the floor, completely clueless on what to do. I cocked the gun and walked up to him, the cross-hairs to his head.

"GIVE ME THE KEYS," I demanded.

He took them out his pocket and dropped them on the floor. I signalled for jenny to come. I presumed the other guys had ran away. We got in the car and drove off. Not looking back.

THE TOP HAT

CATHERINE SPEIRS, YEAR 9

*R*elaxed. Alert. Relaxed. Alert. Not too slow and not too rushed. Anonymous. She tucked a violet strand of hair behind her ear. Her hand brushed the gold star sitting in her ear lobe. She followed the swarm of people. Through underpasses and bridges, on trains and buses.

One man stood. Through the melee of black umbrellas, a top hat stood out. A pair of old welding goggles weighed down on the brim of the hat.

He wanted her to know that this would be a repeat of before: tranquilized again; darkness again; taken again. He had taken her again.

Horns blaring. Lights glaring. A great sign towered over her.

'Welcome'

Her little bubble of astonishment popped as someone shoved her shoulder. She was alone.

'To Fabulous'

Neon signs glowed like portals to unearthly hells. Shining cars pulsed through the streets.

'Las Vegas.'

A heart pumped trucks and taxis as veins stretched in every direction.

Silence. She was back. "No." She had been free. Had she been free? Only one thing would be different this time. She would not escape. She had left her home. This was not her sun. This sun burned her back this sun frowned down on her when no one smiled.

He walked in. Someday she would burn that hat. Someday she would be able to put this behind her.

Quiet people are always seen as weak. Because they don't waste their words, they're forgotten. No one would remember her.

The hat bobbed as it moved towards her, following her through hell. Soon it would catch fire. He might have been a murderer but for that moment she was murderous. The goggles inched closer. She wouldn't see whatever weapon was thirsty for her throat, until she was…

A light flickered behind him. He kept walking. It blinked on and off. Next to the bulb, something glowed red hot. He kept walking. The light burned into her eyes.

"Don't cry pet. I would never let you die so quickly."

"God will take my life, not you."

"After all this time, you still believe someone cares about you."

The light was pulsing round the room now. He pulled those goggles over his eyes. His face was stone. The corner of his mouth twitched. He didn't know what was happening. She had no ideas. This was him, messing with her head. This was him, messing with her mind. Showing who was in control. But he looked too confused for that to be true. A bright ray of light shone through the cracks in the walls. Boom.

She was next to someone. She was slouched on the floor – the floor of something moving. A black boot shifted next to her. Attached to it was a soldier ready to fight. The soldier would win against her. The van lurched backwards as it came to a stop. She was hauled to her feet as what seemed like millions called outside. The doors cracked open slowly as flashes were carried in on the cold night air. Paparazzi screeched and surged towards her. She looked around frantically till she spotted him. Somehow the dreaded hat was untarnished. They dragged her towards a brick building. It swam through her vision as riot police held back the chaotic crowd.

Tensed. Alert. Tensed. Alert. The walls of the corridor, which she was being guided down, was lined with policemen. She reached up to tuck a strand of violet hair behind her ear but stopped short as she remembered her handcuffs. All of her jewellery had been removed, even her star. She followed the swarm of guards to where she was to be tried for murder.

THE MAGIC SOFA BED

LILY BORTHWICK, YEAR 9

From my bedroom window I can see all the way over town to the rolling fields of the hills on the outskirts. It's so... peaceful. And every hour, on the dot, come the church bells ringing away. I can hear them now. Sitting there on my windowsill, just looking out, can distract me from anything.

Suddenly, the church bells change, and there's a ringing sound all around me, like a fire alarm but softer. Echoing around and around the walls. And then I open my eyes. I've always continued my dreams into my alarm, and I can hear it surrounding me, engulfing me through the walls of my dreams but now I am awake, and my bedroom window is far, far away back in my real home, back with my dad. And I'm still stuck here in this old, dingy 'palace', as Mum keeps calling it.

Palace. Could hardly be a palace; its tiny. In my room there's barely enough room for me and my sodding sofa bed.

"Amy! Amy! Dinners ready!"

I go to get up when my sofa bed collapses in on me. I try to struggle out, warring with the cushions, and I can see a little light. Suddenly, I feel the seat give way, and I fall to the floor. But I don't stop when I hit it, I just keep falling. I can see my floor, I fall through it and I'm in the kitchen, but only for a brief second until I break through the wooden floorboards. Just falling and falling and I feel like I will never stop falling. I open my mouth to scream and…

I open my eyes. It's blurry, but I can see where I am. Staring out at that church, and its ringing away. I stand up and walk to my door, it's time for dinner and I can't wait to tell my parents about my weird dream. I pull on the handle but when it opens I'm just staring at the hallway of the new, tiny house. I turn around to look into my room, but as I do it falls away and the ugly, decaying panels replace my beautiful flower wall paper. My desk, bed, all of my shelves full of my photos just disappear, and it's just that horrible, broken sofa bed left.

I run over to it and start kicking it, over and over again, screaming at it, crying, wailing. And there it is. The church bells, as they always do turn to my alarm ringing and ringing around me. It's just a dream, which means I'll still wake up in this godforsaken house. But I'm not waking up like usual; for some reason it's taking so much longer and now I'm just lying on the floor as my alarm grows ever louder. Ringing. Ringing. I have to switch it off. I can't deal with it anymore! I'm just not waking up. I won't open my eyes, I can't. I stand up and start calling out, "Mum! Mum! Please hear me, help!" But no one hears me and my voice just starts echoing along with the alarm.

I run downstairs to the front door and try to open it, but it won't budge. I pull and pull on the handle but it doesn't move. I fumble with the lock but nothing happens. I can't leave this awful house and I can't escape my alarm. This is not some longing dream of my old home with my lovely window; it is my worst nightmare. I run back up to my room through the empty halls and there it is, the only piece of furniture left, the sofa bed. I lie down on it, because if I can fall asleep in my dream it will be over so much quicker. It's freezing cold to the touch and the cushions are almost empty as if they were so old the stuffing had just wasted away. It's so uncomfortable but I'm not awake for long.

I can hear my alarm as I wake up. I sit up and yawn. "Mum I'm up! I've had the worst dream," I shout out down the stairs. I grab the dressing gown hanging up on the back of my door and pull it on. I traipse down the stairs. "Mum! Mum?" But there's no answer. I walk through the kitchen door but its empty. I run back up to her room, but it's empty. She's not in the house anywhere! I keep calling and calling for her but there's no answer. I fall silent, and there it is... the alarm. I'm still in the dream. Now even the few pieces of furniture we've unpacked start disappearing all around me.

For days and days, I've been falling asleep and waking up

here. I don't know quite how long it's been but every time I get up I realise I'm stuck here and I don't know how to escape. And every day I close my eyes and dream within my dream of the view from my old bedroom window. But I can never focus with my alarm going off, constantly reminding me how far I actually am from it. I can only hope I wake up soon but I don't know how... or when.

TRAPPED

JOE WILLIAMS, YEAR 9

*C*old. Still cold. Gingerly, I stepped out from under the ragged, hole-ridden tarpaulin that I called home, I considered what the day would bring. It had all the signs of normality about it. I sat nervously on the cold, stone-hard pavement, wondering whether I would be robbed, even brutally attacked because of my colour, my age, my religion or maybe because I was a desperate beggar who had nothing.

So I sat there. Cold. Bitterly cold. Freezing cold. The harsh winter had started to take its toll on me. I knew that if I didn't move soon, my already fragile body would start shutting down, leaving me at the mercy of the elements – the wind, the rain, the snow. But still I sat there. I had no urge to move. The darkness started to close in on me. One hour became two. Two became five, until eventually it was time to fade back into the greyness of the slums.

"Stop."

I froze to the spot. A feeling shivered down my spine. My muscles tensed. I was ready. Ready to fight whatever threatened me. Cautiously, I turned my body with my clenched fists raised to defend – or strike. But instead of being confronted by a burly mob of thugs, what stood before me was a solitary man. No knife, no gun, just one man. He was well dressed and clean-shaven. I found myself starting to relax. I was not being attacked.

Suddenly, my body slumped. My knees collapsed beneath me. The pain was unbearable. I passed out.

Darkness.

I don't know how long I had been out for, but as I came round I felt completely disorientated, my head shrouded a mist of pain and uncertainty. I looked around, trying to get my bearings. Where was I? What had happened to me? I wanted to get up and run, I needed to find safety, needed to get away from this place. I lifted my head, but a wave of nausea hit me, and I immediately slumped back. I tried again. My body refused to move as if it was not wanting to let me go, not wanting to respond to my urge to flee from wherever I was.

During the next few hours I drifted in and out of consciousness. Each time I came to, I tried again and again to move but it was hopeless. It felt as if my body was tied down, bound to whatever lay beneath it. In the few minutes my body was conscious, I tried to gather my thoughts and work out where I was before I succumbed to yet another surge of nausea and drifted off into a wave of semi-consciousness.

The next time I awoke, it was dark. Time had become irrelevant to me. Once more I tried to will my body to move and get up. Slowly, very slowly, I shifted my frame towards the edge of what I finally realised was a bed. I managed to slide my legs over the side of it so that my body was in a sitting position. Breathe. Just breathe. Slowly. Don't rush. My body felt weak and it wasn't responding how I wanted it to. I could feel another wave of nausea rising up within me, but I pushed it down with the little strength that I had.

Concentrate.

Think.

My eyes traced the outline of the room and fixed on a door, a door I hadn't noticed before. This was my means of escape, but then without warning a shaft of light appeared round the doorframe, as if someone the other side had read my thoughts. I heard footsteps approaching, moving closer towards the door with every second that passed.

The handle creaked as it began to turn.

I took a sharp intake of breath, my pulse racing, my heart beating more furiously than ever before. It seemed to take an age before it opened. My hands gripped the bedsheet. Whatever was on the other side would determine my fate. Whether it was good or evil, I couldn't move.

I was trapped.

FLATLINE

AMBER NEIL, YEAR 9

*E*veryday: Get up. Eat food. Get dressed. Clean teeth. Brush hair. Go to work. Go home. Eat food. Get changed. Clean teeth. Brush hair. Go to sleep. There is nothing, until...

Today.

Sitting, staring. A photo of friends. Just one small photo can fill a person with so many bad memories. Sad, alone. Just one small photo can make someone want to forget. Violet looked at the slanted clock once more and found herself running for her shoes. *One more time and you're out*, she thought; her boss was circling her mind. She contemplated her job as she scrambled for her keys and left, locking the door with the spare key under her doormat. She ran down the stairs of the building and got into the car as her phone vibrated. It was her boyfriend Duncan asking where she was. How could she forget their anniversary breakfast?

Driving, as usual, Violet went the same route as she normally did. She looked at the time. One glance of a clock can make one's foot push down on the accelerator more than they need.

There was a screeching of rubber along the road and then a deafening silence.

Beep, beep. Flatline. Her heart skipped one too many times. Tears were shed.... but... prematurely, it seemed. Violet's precious heart started beating. It was a miracle.

VIOLET

I wake up not knowing where or who I am. I try to put some words together, but I can't remember how. The doctors keep showing me all these photos but I just can't remember what they are. Just one small photo can make someone want to remember.

Everyday. Wake up. Eat. Sleep. Repeat. Until.

I am allowed to go home – well, to my parents.

Being surrounded by 'familiar' faces makes me so angry. If I can't remember them, they don't exist to me, so why should they exist to anyone? I ask for a cup of water, to excuse myself to the kitchen. I try to resist but my anger is too strong, subtly, I search the kitchen for an object that can be used as a weapon. A sharp, gleaming knife glows as I feel the blade with my finger. Perfect. A lightning bolt of fear struck my mother's pale face. She can't anticipate my plans – I don't know them myself and I allow myself to be led to the seat overlooking the garden. Suddenly it's all camomile tea and calming view as I hear her calling for the emergency services from the kitchen.

I can feel myself receding, fading into the distance as if in a long tunnel. I watch my progress towards the open door of the ambulance, feel the soft touch of blankets and hear the reassuringly soothing voices of hi-vis figures.

And then I notice someone. He has the purest of eyes watching me with a silver lined tear rolling down his cheek. My heart flutters as he approaches. People are shouting at him to stay away, but he carries on walking towards me.

His eyes are staring into mine. Reaching for my soul, as if he has the key. I remember him. He strokes my face and everything comes flooding back to me... Duncan. I run, taking the back entrance from the garden into a maze of side streets. I want to go home – my home.

Now. I pick up a pen and slowly start to write on a scrap of paper.

DUNCAN

I followed after her, frantically twisting and turning down alleys, tripping over my own two feet up the stairs. By the time I got to her flat she had locked the door, only God knows what she was doing.

I broke the door to a note. I was in tears when I read the contents. "Now it's time for me to move on too. I finally know what I've got to do. Hope you find someone beautiful. You were the light in my darkness, you helped me find the truth, and I just want to say...thank you." I turn over the small note and continue to read. "Gone to weigh my soul. Don't try to stop me because I know I've got to go. You watched me turn cold, but you won't watch me grow old."

Holding the note close to my heart, I knew that it was too late when I try opening the bathroom door. Water snaked from under the door, highlights of red chasing it.

THE ABYSS OF THE MOON

CHARLIE NEWMAN YEAR 9

I am suddenly awake, disturbed by the noise of Zach starting a conversation. I can't sleep any longer. As soon as he says anything, my will to sleep is gone, though I feel I shouldn't get out of bed tonight. I avert my eyes from the ceiling to the monitor. Zach asks if I am awake and I reply that his message woke me up.

Zach isn't very calm this night. He seems panicked. He tells me to switch to Channel 58. The channel seems decent enough for a news channel but that doesn't last. It goes to an emergency message. It's a weather warning. The event has little to inform me what is going on, which makes me more worried. It goes back to normal programming without a tone explaining the broadcast is over. Zach and I are puzzled. I try to ask him questions to see if he understands the situation, but he has grown silent. My questions only grow as the programming continues. It seems fine… for merely seconds. It goes back to the message and it seems the event has only worsened. It has a become a full-scale civil danger.

It only gets worse when the messages seem to be hijacked, telling us to face the danger and give ourselves up to them. It seems like a battle between the news station and the hijackers. And the station fails to reinstate the planned broadcasting. I take the messages seriously. Do not look up, face away from mirrors and do not come in contact with moonlight. I block the windows over with blankets and barricade the doors with anything I can find. I hear screaming coming from somewhere outside. The channel tries to explain that whatever hijacked the channel was a false alarm and the whole situation is a hoax. Zach speaks again.

"Did you look at the moon?"

"What do you mean? The whole thing was a hoax!"

He replies to me, "Was it?"

I check outside. It wasn't a hoax. White creatures. White eyes like the moon. Tearing through people's skin like razor blades. I used to be afraid of the Light. Now I am afraid of the Dark as well. What can I do now? Sit and wait like my father?

He was a coward in my mother's eyes. He gave in to people's commands and fell straight into a well of torture. We'd hide from the assaulters whilst my father would point a gun to his own head. Thinking of this gives me a frightful idea.

And the broadcast gives more and more trepidation with more messages playing. However, it seems like a genuine message. I keep watching it while the creatures start to break down my door.

The message stops.

ACKNOWLEDGMENTS

With thanks to Mrs C Swaisland, project leader, and the dedicated teachers of Guildford County School English Department.

ABOUT THE YOUNG AUTHOR PROJECT

The Young Author Project is run by a small, independent team and we love what we do. We have a combined 25 years' experience in publishing, writing, and teaching so putting together the Young Author Project has been a labour of love.

Our Director, Cara Thurlbourn says:

"When I was at school, I was desperate to be an author - but the notion seemed far fetched, unachievable and something that only the lucky few could master.

Today, things are very different. Advances in technology have made it possible for anyone who is passionate about writing to become a successful author.

Our goal with the Young Author Project is to show students who love to write but think they're not good enough, or that it won't lead anywhere, that it can.

We want to empower young writers and turn them into young authors, and we believe that this, in turn, will fuel their love of books, their academic writing skills, their confidence and their sense of self-worth."

To find out more about the Young Author Project, please visit www.youngauthorproject.com.

25027926R00111

Printed in Great Britain
by Amazon